wish you were dead

TODD STRASSER

EGMONT
USA

NEW YORK

EGMONT

We bring stories to life

First published by Egmont USA, 2009
443 Park Avenue South, Suite 806
New York, NY 10016

Copyright © Todd Strasser, 2009
All rights reserved

1 3 5 7 9 8 6 4 2

www.egmontusa.com
www.toddstrasser.com

Library of Congress Cataloging-in-Publication Data

Strasser, Todd.
Wish you were dead / Todd Strasser.
p. cm.
Summary: Madison, a senior at a suburban New York high school, tries to uncover who is responsible for the disappearance of her friends, popular students mentioned in the posts of an anonymous blogger, while she, herself is being stalked online and in-person.
ISBN 978-1-60684-007-8 (hardcover) — ISBN 978-1-60684-049-8 (lib. bdg.) [1.Missing persons—Fiction. 2. Kidnapping—Fiction. 3. High schools—Fiction. 4. Schools—Fiction. 5. Stalking—Fiction. 6. Blogs—Fiction. 7. New York (State)—Fiction.] I. Title.
PZ7.S899Wj 2009
[Fic]—dc22
2009014641

Printed in the United States of America

To the folks at Egmont,
who I hope will all live
long and joyous lives.

Str-S-d #1

Today at school Lucy Cunningham looked at me like I was something the cat coughed up. I don't have to explain who Lucy is. You already know, because there's only one kind of girl who would look at anyone that way. I'm going to be completely honest here because this is my new blog, so what's the point of pretending? So here goes. It really hurts when Lucy looks at me that way. But here's what hurts even more. Sometimes when people look at me that way, I feel like maybe they're right.

....

💬 0 Comments

Str-S-d #2

I hate myself. I know I'm not supposed to say that. I'm supposed to say that deep down I know I'm a really good person and only shallow people care about appearances. Well, I guess deep down I'm really shallow because I would give anything not to look like me. Why couldn't I have been born pretty? Or really smart and clever? Or talented? Anything.

··

💬 2 Comments

ApRilzDay said...

Hello? WOW, I just read your blog. Hey, I don't know you, but I really wish you felt better about yourself. I mean, don't YOU believe everyone has something good about themselves? And you ARE talented. That line about deep down you're really shallow is FUNNY.

Str-S-d said...

It is? I didn't mean it that way. But thanks anyway, I guess.

Str-S-d #3

This girl once asked me why I didn't at least wear nicer clothes. That's what she said: "at least." As if it bothered her that I didn't even try. Not that my mom has the money. But that's not the real answer. The real answer is: Do you know what would happen if I tried to wear nicer clothes to school? They'd say, "Oh, look at her. She's trying to fix herself up. How hopeless is that?" Why do they have to be so mean and catty?

....

💬 3 Comments

Realgurl4013 said...
> Cause theyre totally inseeecure and need 2 find someone 2 dump on so people wont dump on them.

ApRilzDay said...
> It really isn't about what THEY think. It's about what YOU think. Wearing nice new things makes ME feel good. I mean, I guess I do care what other people think. But it's really for ME. Maybe you could TRY it once and see what happens? You might be surprised.

Str-S-d said...
> I guess I could try.

Str-S-d #4

I want to die. I would kill myself right now if I had the guts. Today I did something nice with my hair and wore this cute top my aunt got me for my birthday and . . . God, I can't believe I did this . . . a padded bra? And they laughed. You know how they bunch up in the hall and stare at you, then turn to each other and laugh and keep glancing at you to make sure you know it's you they're laughing at? I just wanted to die, vanish, evaporate, cease to exist. And the worst thing was I was stuck there. At least until lunch. Then I went home and changed. I didn't know how I could go back to school, but then I remembered my mom had this medicine for when she gets really upset. It's not like it gets you high or anything. So I figured, just this once. It helped a little.

. . . .

💬 4 comments

Realgurl4013 said...

Hey, hey, I say, whatever gets you through the day day, is Oh-Oh-Okay.

4204ever said...

Doesn't get you high? Then what's the point?

ApRilzDay said...

Seriously? I'm so sorry that happened! I mean, I feel like it's partly MY fault for suggesting it. But at least YOU were BRAVE enough to try, right? Maybe if you keep doing it they'll get used to it and not even notice anymore.

Str-S-d said...

You can't be serious. Try again? You obviously don't have a clue how horrible it feels.

Str-S-d #5

It's taken me a long time to get to this point. I said I was being honest in this blog, but I wasn't completely because I didn't say what I was really thinking. I mean, wishing people would die. That's how I really feel most of the time. I just wish they would die. I didn't write it before because I tell myself I shouldn't feel that way. But the more I try to rid myself of these thoughts, the stronger they grow. So forget trying to be nice. Forget trying to pretend. Those people have made my life miserable. I want them to die.

I'll begin with Lucy. She is definitely first on the list. You can't believe how it feels to be in the cafeteria and turn around and there she is staring at me like I'm some disgusting bug or vermin. Does she really think I WANT to be this way? I hate you, Lucy. I really hate you. You are my #1 pick. I wish you were dead.

....

💬 5 Comments

Realgurl4013 said...
I know just how you feel. Popular kids suuuck.

Ru22cool? said...
Did it ever occur to you to try and improve your looks instead of just being a crybaby complainer?

Str-S-d said...
Go read Str-S-d #4, Ru22.

IaMnEmEsIs said...
Perhaps your wish will come true.

ApRilzDay said...
I'm sorry, but I think this is REALLY wrong. I know they were really nasty mean to you the other day, but you have to realize that it's just because THEY'RE the stupid and immature ones. But wishing someone would die is really wrong. Really.

chapter 1

Sunday 3:09 A.M.

THE RED TAILLIGHTS of Tyler Starling's ugly purple car disappeared into the dark. It was just after three A.M., chilly and quiet. Lucy Cunningham stepped off her front walk and strolled down the dark tree-lined street. The last thing she needed was for her father to look through the bedroom window and see her smoking.

Lucy hugged herself, her thin jacket not warm enough in the crisp November air. Except for a few lights above front doors, the houses on her block were dark. In the sky above, stars sparkled through the bare tree branches. It was almost eerily silent, but Lucy was too busy thinking about the fight she'd just had with Adam to notice.

On the surface, the argument had been about the future. She wanted to apply to Stanford. But Adam was dead set on Harvard. Being both an excellent lacrosse goalie and a straight-A student with 2300 boards, he had a very good chance of being accepted. But why couldn't he also apply to Stanford? Their lacrosse team was better than Harvard's.

She took a drag. The cigarette glowed red-hot as tobacco

turned to ash and smoke filled her lungs in that strangely soothing way she seemed to crave more and more lately. Just as she had begun to look forward to drinking every Friday and Saturday night. Yes, she'd been warned not to drink while on her meds. Yes, she'd been told a thousand times that smoking kills. But after a fight like the one she'd just had with Adam, how could she *not*?

Lucy shivered. *Don't pretend*, she told herself. The real issue between Adam and her wasn't college. It was about Adam ending their relationship. She'd been losing him for months and, distracted by school and SATs and college garbage, hadn't even noticed. But there was no doubt in her mind that tonight he'd begun to lay the groundwork for a breakup. How? By making sure she saw what she'd failed to see before—that there was someone else.

Lucy cursed herself for being so blind. Why hadn't she figured it out sooner? Adam had lost interest. Even being extra sweet and attentive tonight, and touching him in all the right places hadn't worked. So it was time to switch to damage-control mode. No boy had ever dumped her before, and it wasn't going to happen now. She would simply have to dump him first . . . right now. As soon as she went inside she would post it on Facebook so that the evidence of it . . . the *timing* of it . . . would be there for everyone to see. And then she would apply to Stanford. She wouldn't give in to Adam. She had always *been* a winner, would always *be* a winner. And winners did whatever it took not to lose. So good-bye, Adam Pinter.

Lucy crushed the butt of the cigarette with her shoe. No matter what her problems, she could overcome them. It was a matter of will. If you worked hard enough, you could do anything. Whatever Lucy was, she'd willed herself to become.

She'd worked for it, suffered for it, agonized, and fought for it. If it meant cheating on a test to get the highest grade, she did it. If it meant stealing someone's boyfriend because he was the hottest guy in the class, she did that, too. And this is just the start. After all, high school was nothing more than potty training for life.

Lost in thought, Lucy turned back through the dark silence toward her house. The tall trees cast skeletal night shadows. The quiet hung in the air around her like mist. Despite the solitude of the late hour, it never occurred to Lucy to feel nervous. This was Soundview, the best of neighborhoods, the place where she'd grown up and had always felt safe.

As she passed a wide tree that cast a thick, spidery shadow across the street, a figure quietly stepped out. Lucy never saw or heard a thing. The presence moved up behind her, barely disturbing the still air. From out of nowhere, a damp rag smelling strongly chemical was jammed hard against her nose and mouth. Alarm instantly raced from Lucy's core to her extremities. Her hands flew to her face and tried to tear the rag away, but that first breath of chemicals brought a fog to her brain, making her reactions sluggish. She flailed feebly at the strong gloved hands holding the rag, but her fingers seemed unable to grip. By the time she tried to scream, she'd taken a second breath, and the cry that left her throat, muffled by the rag, was so weak and faint that it sounded like the bleating of some distant forlorn animal.

The heavy fog was like a trapdoor pressing down on her consciousness.

Her knees gave out.

She went limp.

Her body would have collapsed in a heap were it not for the arms that went around her chest. Her attacker began to drag her around the corner to a parked car.

Lucy Cunningham's heels scraped along the dark, quiet street . . . and all her worries about the future became a thing of the past.

Sunday 3:02 A.M. (7 minutes earlier)

"RICH BITCH," TYLER Starling muttered as he steered with one hand and turned up the music with the other. It was something he called hard-style techno, which, he claimed, was very popular in Germany and the Netherlands.

Next to him in the dark car, I winced. The loud thumping music was raw electronic and difficult to follow. An assault on the ears, especially given the late hour, it only added to the discomfort I was already feeling. All week I'd looked forward to spending tonight with this new, interesting guy who'd suddenly shown up at Soundview High almost a month after school began. He was tall, wiry, handsome, and, I thought, seriously sexy, with a slightly crooked nose that must have been the result of being broken.

But now, as the final moments of our night together approached, my plans were slipping away into disappointment. Tyler's "rich bitch" comment just made it worse. If he didn't like rich people, I was in serious trouble.

There were other reasons to feel discomfort. By dropping Lucy Cunningham off in front of her house and driving away, we'd broken an important Safe Rides rule—making sure "the client" was safely inside before we left. But it was nearly three A.M., and Lucy was being a complete pain, standing in the street and refusing to go into her house. What were we supposed to do? Take her by the hand and lead her to the front door?

"She's not like that most of the time," I said.

"Why are you making excuses for her?" Tyler asked as he drove.

"Because I've known her for a long time. In fact, in middle school, we were best friends."

"That doesn't give her the right to dump on us." Tyler craned his neck for the street signs that would lead us out of Lucy's neighborhood.

Twenty minutes earlier, we'd picked her up at Cassandra Quinn's house. It was just after two thirty, and through the brightly lit windows we could see that the party was still going strong. The front door had opened and Lucy stumbled across the lawn with the unsteady gait of someone who'd been intimate with Jell-O shots. I was surprised by that, considering the medications she was taking. And why had she called Safe Rides instead of rolling with Adam?

She opened the back door and got in. "Take me home," she grumbled. "And make it snappy."

Tyler started to drive, the hard-style techno blaring.

"Would you turn that crap off?" Lucy demanded.

Tyler turned the music down, but not off. I heard a telltale rustle from the backseat. Lucy had placed a cigarette in her lips.

"No smoking, Lucy," I said.

"Drop dead," she grumbled, and searched her bag for a light.

Tyler looked at her in the rearview mirror. "Keep smoking and you'll beat us to it."

Lucy harrumphed as she pulled out a green plastic lighter and thumbed it. A flame shot up. She lit the cigarette, rolled the window halfway down, and exhaled. Cold November air rushed into the car. I tightened my red cashmere scarf around my neck.

"Could anything be more pathetic than this?" Lucy muttered. "Why are you chauffeuring people around on a Saturday night?"

"It's my community-service requirement," I said. "How was the party anyway?"

"Beside the huge fight I had with Adam?" Lucy said. "It sucked. Same old, same old, except for some FCC creeps. I so cannot wait for high school to end."

We rode in silence until Lucy looked into the rearview mirror and caught Tyler's eye. "I know you. You're the one who wears that black trench coat and always sits by yourself at lunch. A regular social butterfly."

Tyler stared back at her for what seemed longer than necessary. I felt an unexpected stab of jealousy. Like a starlet in one of those old black-and-white movies, Lucy was the beautiful blonde sitting in the shadows, smoking. The one who always got the hero. And knew what to do with him, too. Meanwhile, all I'd wanted all night was for Tyler to look at me the way he'd just looked at Lucy.

"Tyler, please watch where you're going," I said.

"You heard her, Tyler," Lucy added from the back. "Be a good little boy; eyes on the road."

A few moments later we stopped in front of Lucy's house, a large white colonial rising up behind a broad swath of carefully manicured lawn, speckled with orange, yellow, and brown leaves.

Lucy got out without a "thank you" and banged the car door closed. She took a few steps up the path, then stopped and turned with an annoyed frown on her face.

I opened my window. "We're supposed to make sure everyone goes inside."

For no apparent reason other than pure orneriness, Lucy held up the lighter and lit a second cigarette, crossed her arms, and gazed up at the stars while she exhaled.

I closed the window and turned to Tyler. "Maybe we should go."

"You sure?" he asked.

It was almost three in the morning and hard to imagine that Lucy was going anywhere except inside. I was tired and disappointed that nothing had developed with Tyler. Now I just wanted to get into bed. "She's just being obstinate. I bet she'll go inside the second we leave."

We drove away, leaving Lucy standing in front of her house. Tyler turned the bad music back up. In no time it was giving me a headache.

"Tyler, I'm sorry to say this. Maybe it's the time of night, and I'm just really drained, but that music is so hard to take," I said. "Is it totally obnoxious of me to ask if you'd turn it down?"

"Not at all." He turned it off. Not just down the way he had for Lucy. So maybe that was a hopeful sign and the evening wasn't a total loss after all. I glanced at his profile and thought about his personality—independent, confident, and more worldly than most guys his age. He'd told me earlier that it had taken him two years of working after school to save up for his car. It was hard to think of anyone else I knew who'd bought his or her own car. In Soundview most of the kids got one from their parents the moment they passed their driver's test.

"Make a right here," I said with a yawn when we got to Bayside Way. Tyler turned onto the narrow road, passing driveways that disappeared into dark woods. I thought again about his "rich bitch" comment and wasn't surprised that his forehead furrowed when we stopped at a small white guardhouse with a gate. With a cautious squint, the guard inside slid open the window and leaned forward, peering at the unfamiliar car. When he saw me in the passenger seat, a smile of relief appeared on his lips. "Oh, good evening, Miss Archer."

"Hi, Joe," I said.

The guard slid the window closed and raised the gate. Tyler drove through. "Miss Archer?" he repeated.

"It's just a formality."

"That's his moonlighting job when he's not being a cop?"

Surprised, I said, "How did you know he was a policeman?"

"I can smell 'em."

"Sounds like you don't like the police."

Tyler didn't respond. We were on Premium Point now, a gated community on a thin strip of land that jutted out into the Sound, lined with what could only be described as estates. Tyler drove slowly, peering at the dark silhouettes of vast lawns and large houses.

"I'm down at the end," I said.

A moment later he stopped in the circular driveway and stared through the windshield at the vast stone facade of the place I called home. I had a feeling that he, too, was thinking back to his "rich bitch" comment. I felt bad. I'd had high hopes for us connecting this evening, even going so far as to fantasize ending it with a kiss. But maybe I'd hoped for too much. All we'd done was share a car for Safe Rides, which didn't exactly qualify as a hot date.

"Thanks for driving me home." I reached for my backpack.

"Wait." Tyler turned to me. I looked back at him in the dark and felt a shiver of anticipation. Was he going to say that he liked me? That he had also been looking forward all week to this evening?

But all he said was, "I'm sorry. I didn't know."

He didn't have to explain what he was sorry about. We both knew.

"You don't have to be sorry," I said. "It's just . . . Things aren't always what they seem, okay? Maybe not everyone who's rich is a bitch."

"I didn't say they were," Tyler said. "I only said Lucy was. I . . . I don't think you're a bitch at all. In fact, I think you're pretty nice."

"Thank you, Tyler," I said, and thought, *Maybe the night wasn't a total loss after all.*

I got out of the car and let myself through the heavy wooden door into the house, temporarily disabling the alarm system to give me time to get up to my room. Upstairs, even though I could barely keep my eyes open, it was impossible to go to bed without first checking my messages, and that was where I found the latest from PBleeker, my cyberstalker:

I once heard you say you hated how cliquey school was, but I

bet you'd never go out with someone like me. You always act
like you're open-minded and sensitive, but I wonder if, just
like everyone else, you judge people by their looks. I know
you're not stuck up like some of those other kids, because
you're always nice and talk to everyone. But how come you
only hang out with the people in the most popular clique?

I shivered and turned away from my laptop, wishing that just
this once I hadn't checked my messages before going to bed. *I
once heard you say . . . You always act like . . .* Was PBleeker
someone who knew me *that* well, or was that just part of the
mind game he (or was PBleeker a *she*?) played? All I knew was
that for the past year, PBleeker's presence in my life had become
one more curse, like my period, college applications, and zits.

I went to bed with the disturbed and uncomfortable feeling
that always followed a PBleeker message. Sometimes they kept
me awake for hours. But not tonight. At least the evening with
Tyler had ended on a positive note. And that, plus my over-
whelming fatigue, helped me drift off.

chapter 3

Oh, poor, poor Lucy, look at you cowering in the corner with your face and hands streaked with dirt and your pretty blonde hair bedraggled and your makeup all smeared. It doesn't smell very nice in there, does it? We've gotten used to it. But then, we've never been accustomed to the finer things in life the way you have.

Please don't grovel and beg. We know your father is a doctor and has lots of money, but don't you understand? It's not about money. That's not the point. Your medications? No, I'm so sorry, but that's not something we have here. Really, Lucy, it's so unbecoming for a young woman of your stature to cry and plead. Look at it this way. You've had it so good for so many years. Surely at some point everyone pays the price, don't you think? Isn't it only fair? You caused so many so much pain. Now you'll get to see how the other half lives.

Oh, did we say "lives"?

Sorry.

Str-S-d #6

There was supposed to be a big party last night. I know because they were talking about it at school on Friday. They know you're not invited and then they talk about it loud in the hall when you pass and look to see how you react. I haven't been invited to a party since sixth grade, so you'd think they'd realize that I'm used to it. At this point, I wouldn't go to a party even if I was invited. Life sucks. People suck. Don't tell me I have a bad attitude or that things will get better someday. You're not me. You don't know what it's like.

....

💬 3 comments

ApRilzDay said...
I'm sorry you feel that way.

IaMnEmEsIs said...
You're not alone. We know what it's like.

One4therOd said...
Pathetic self-pitying whiner.

* * *

TYLER IS DRIVING. It's so dark that all I can see is the short stretch of road racing toward us beneath the headlights. Tyler is leaning over to kiss me. I like the feel of his lips on mine, but shouldn't he pull over? It's too dark to drive and kiss. But I'm afraid he'll get mad if I ask him to stop kissing me and watch the road. Tyler, it's not that I don't want you to kiss me. Really. I just don't want to crash. Tyler, my parents will be really upset if we die. Tyler, please open your eyes and watch where you're going.

Open your eyes. . . .

Please.

My cell phone was ringing. I opened my eyes and looked at the clock on the night table. 10:34. All at once I was both relieved and disappointed. Thank God it was a dream, darn it! Tyler wasn't kissing me, but he wasn't driving and not watching where he was going, either.

The phone rang again. I picked it up and stared blearily at the number. It was Courtney. "What happened to our 'No Calls Before Noon' rule?" I answered with a yawn.

"This can't wait," she said. "Like, Lucy Cunningham's parents are calling her friends, looking for her? Turns out she didn't come home last night. Did you hear anything?"

"Hear what? When?" I asked.

"Like, last night? Didn't you and Tyler drive her home?"

"Yes, but—"

"But she didn't get there, okay? Jen Waits just called me."

My thoughts drifted back to the previous night and my last glimpse of Lucy, standing stubbornly on her front walk with her arms crossed. My heart staggered and skipped. *We didn't wait to watch her go inside.*

"Did Lucy say anything?" Courtney asked.

"About what?"

"I don't know. Just anything."

Outside my room, footsteps came up the stairs, rapidly. *Rap! Rap!* Knocks on my bedroom door. "Madison?" Mom came in, holding the portable phone. The tips of her blonde hair were wet, which slightly darkened the shoulders of her white terry-cloth robe. Her hand was over the phone's speaker.

"Later," I said into my cell phone and snapped it shut.

"Did you drive Lucy home last night?" Mom asked, worry lines joining the reddened bathing-cap line in her forehead.

I nodded. It wasn't hard to guess who was on the phone. My parents and the Cunninghams had been close friends for years. The frown on Mom's face deepened and she held the phone to her ear. "Paul? Yes, she drove Lucy home last night. Uh-huh. Uh-huh. Yes, I understand." Mom handed the phone to me. "He wants to speak to you."

I took the phone. Everything was happening too fast, and it left me feeling shaky and uncertain. "Hello?"

"Madison?" Lucy's father sounded grave and urgent as he explained what I already knew—Lucy hadn't come home the night before. "Can you tell me where and what time you dropped her off?"

"Right at your front walk around three."

"Did she say she was going anywhere else? Or meeting anyone?"

"No."

"Did she start up the walk toward the house?"

"Not really," I said. "She just stood there smoking a cigarette."

This information was met with silence. I suddenly felt guilty and added, "She only does it at parties sometimes."

"Had she been drinking?" Dr. Cunningham asked.

"Yes, I'm pretty sure."

Lucy's father muttered to himself. "Did she say *anything* that might have indicated that she didn't plan on going right into the house?" Anxiety and hope slithered through his words.

"No. She just seemed really upset. I mean, have you talked to Adam?"

"Yes," Dr. Cunningham replied tersely. "Did you happen to see anyone else around when you dropped her off?" A hint of desperation tinted the edges of his voice.

"No. It was really late. I don't remember seeing anyone. I'm really sorry."

"There's nothing to be sorry about, Madison. Just promise me that if you do remember anything else, anything at all, you'll call me immediately."

"I will," I said. "I promise." I hung up and handed the phone to Mom.

"You're sure there isn't something you're not—" she began.

"Mom, give me some credit, okay?"

She sighed. "You're right. I shouldn't have said that. Those poor people. I feel so terrible for them. They must be worried sick."

Once again, I replayed the memory of Lucy standing in the dark, hugging herself against the chill, her cigarette glowing. Where could she have gone?

"Well, hopefully she's safe." Mom checked her watch. "You remember that your father's expecting you to crew for him this afternoon?"

I'd forgotten. "Who're we racing against?"

"American, I think."

The American Yacht Club was on the other side of the Sound. "We won't be back until after dark. I have homework."

"Take it with you," Mom said, heading for the door.

I slid back down into the covers and squeezed Rumpy, my ratty old Gund dog. My thoughts drifted back again to the night before. What could have happened? Where could Lucy have possibly gone? Nothing I could think of made sense. And yet, I couldn't shake the feeling that it was my fault.

It was dark when *Time Off*, Dad's racing sloop, returned to its slip. The other members of the crew had families and Sunday dinners to get back to, and it wasn't long before Dad and I were left alone to finish the job of packing up and securing the boat. On Sundays Mom was used to keeping dinner warm until we could get home.

"Get your homework done?" Dad asked as we tied the mainsail to the boom. It had gone from a cool but breezy and sunny afternoon to a chilly, damp, dark evening. My hands were cold and a little stiff. I wished I was wearing gloves.

"Uh-huh." I'd done my homework at the galley table below

decks while Dad and the other crew members sailed home after the race.

He smiled. "I know crewing wasn't your first choice today, Maddy, but it makes me happy when you come along."

"No prob, Dad." I was always glad to spend time with him. These Sunday-afternoon races were his only respite from his role as head of M. Archer and Company, his investment firm. There were often entire weeks when I didn't see him. Dad literally traveled the world to attend meetings, meet investors, and consider business possibilities. On any given day he might be in Brazil looking at sugarcane producers, then fly overnight to meet a wealthy sheik in Dubai for a breakfast meeting, and then continue to Vietnam to look at a toy-manufacturing facility.

The smile on my father's face was replaced by a pensive look. "I hope they've found Lucy by now."

"Me, too," I said. But I could not shake the sense of dread that I'd felt all day. An hour before, we'd called Mom from the boat to see if there was any news. There wasn't. Lucy was still missing.

By the time we finished securing the mainsail, a crescent moon had risen over the Sound, creating a shimmering white swath of moonlight across the black waters. Dad and I walked through the dark boatyard past the tall, hulking cranes and hoists, the dry-docked hulls, and racks of powerboats. We'd almost reached the parking lot when I realized I'd left my books in *Time Off*'s galley. I told Dad I'd only be a moment, then rushed back through the dark.

Walking quickly through the shadows left by the tall white hulls, the only sound I heard was the crunch of my footsteps on the gravel. I reached the ramp that led down to the dock and hur-

ried along, my thunking footsteps now accompanied by the slosh
of water. A few moments later I climbed on board the *Time Off*,
dashed into the galley, and grabbed my backpack. While lock-
ing the galley door, I thought I heard footsteps on the dock and
stretched up to look out at the dark. But there was no one on the
dock, just the empty berths and the sticklike silhouette of a mast
here and there.

Pulling my backpack over my shoulder, I walked quickly along
the dock, water sloshing beneath me with every step, my eyes darting left and right. *Stop it*, I told myself. *There's nothing wrong.
You're just freaked by what's going on with Lucy.* Reaching the end,
I hurried up the metal ramp and once again started through the
boatyard. Something felt odd, but it took several moments for me
to realize what it was. Abruptly I stopped and listened. At first all
I could hear was the thumping of my own heart and the clinks of
halyards knocking against metal masts, but I was certain there'd
been another sound, almost an echo of my own footsteps.

Stop it! You're just imaging things. I tried to reassure myself,
but it didn't stop the nervousness from creeping up my spine.
Once again I told myself I was being silly. There was nothing to
be afraid of—except maybe Dad's impatience if I didn't get back
to the car soon.

I started to walk again but almost immediately heard the
echoing footsteps. I stopped. Was it only the echo of my own steps
bouncing off the broad white hulls around me? Or was it something else? Was there someone walking parallel to me one line of
boat hulls over?

My heart was rattling and I could hear my own shallow

breaths. *This is stupid,* I told myself. *There's nothing to be afraid of.* I took a tentative step, then stopped to listen. This time there was no echo. I took another. Still no echo. I began to walk.

There it was again . . . footsteps crunching . . . and they weren't mine.

I started to run.

Now the footsteps were louder, accompanied by the scattering of gravel sent flying by my rapidly moving feet. In the clatter it was impossible to distinguish my steps from anyone else's, and I pictured someone gaining on me from behind. Hands reaching out to grab me. The need to scream gathered in my chest, but just then I reached the parking lot.

Dad was waiting by the car.

"You didn't have to run," he said.

I wasn't so sure. Breathing hard, heart banging in my chest, I looked back at the boatyard and saw nothing but shadows, and the hulls of dry-docked boats. But there'd been someone back there. I was certain of it.

chapter 4

Monday 7:43 A.M.

Did you say something, Lucy? You're thirsty? Oh, Lucy,
really now, we don't think you're in a position to
complain. Sorry? Of course they're looking for you.
Yes, they surely will find you . . . sooner or later.
We're sure your parents are doing everything within
their power. But let's be honest, Lucy. Except for your
parents, do you really think there's anyone who's truly
upset that you're gone?

Oh, Lucy, we really don't think you should have said
that. No, no, it's much too late to say you're sorry.

*　*　*

ON MONDAY MORNING I pulled my Audi into Courtney's driveway. My parents had given me the choice of any car I wanted as long as it had front and side airbags. I'd thought the Audi was cute.

Courtney was always late, but I was used to that and had stopped at Starbucks for a venti caramel macchiato. I opened the window, smelled the scent of cool salt air, and sipped my coffee. The Rajwars lived in a sprawling split-level house with a pool and tennis court in the backyard that were hardly ever used. Parked in a corner of the driveway near the garage was Courtney's VW Bug with a light green tarp over it. She'd lost her license after being caught speeding twice within six months of passing her road test. Now she would have to wait until she was twenty-one to drive.

Courtney came out wearing black-and-white horizontal-striped leggings, a pink satin skirt, and a thick, baggy green turtle-neck sweater. Her black hair had streaks of blonde and pink and she had a tiny diamond stud in one nostril. She was a gorgeous girl with olive skin and dark, almond-shaped eyes.

"S'up?" she said, getting into the car and taking the caramel macchiato out of my hand for a swig. "Yum." She looked around. "Got anything to eat?"

"Do you want to get something from your house before we go?" I asked.

"Like, there's nothing to eat in there?" Courtney said. "I haven't seen my father in days. I don't even know if he's here or away on a business trip?"

Courtney's mom was back in Chandigarh, the town in India

where she'd been born, caring for Courtney's sick grandmother. Her father worked for a big international corporation and traveled even more than my father. Courtney's older sister, Abigail, was studying at NYU Law, and was supposed to keep an eye on her younger sister while her parents were away, but Abby spent most of her time at her boyfriend's apartment in the city. As a result, Courtney was the least supervised person I knew.

"So . . . heard anything more about Lucy?" I asked as I backed the Audi out of the driveway.

Courtney shook her head and fiddled with her iPod. To my surprise, she offered no opinion. Sometimes she could be Little Miss Motormouth, so I had to wonder why she was being so quiet. She scrolled through her iPod and definitely wasn't acting like herself. We'd known each other and had been part of the same crowd for a couple of years, but only recently had we started to become friends. Admittedly, we were an odd pairing. I was petite and blonde (well, streaked blonde) with a turned-up nose, athletic, and, I admit, something of a bookish Goody Two-shoes homebody. Courtney was tall and lithe, dark and exotic, utterly disinterested in sports, not the greatest student, and had a rep for being wildly social and socially wild. What few people knew, mostly because Courtney didn't care to let them know, was that when she felt like it, she could be really smart and perceptive. The first time we had a seriously deep conversation, she told me she'd always thought I was too reserved and "intellectual," and too much of a prude (does anyone besides Courtney still use that word?). I admitted that I'd thought she was kind of superficial and maybe even a little slutty (although that was based more on rumor than firsthand observation).

"Oh!" In the seat next to me, Courtney suddenly thought of something and turned down the volume on her iPod. "What happened with Tyler?"

"Less than I'd hoped," I said with a shrug.

My friend pouted sympathetically. "Sparks didn't fly?"

"Not even close. I don't know, Courts. I'm just so bad at flirting." The truth was, I was bad at just about *everything* when it came to guys. I was comfortable talking to them about serious things—school, social causes, the environment—but the moment any aspect of romance was introduced, I instantly lost my bearings and tended to freeze up with self-conscious uncertainty.

"Did you touch his arm when you talked to him?" she asked.

It felt a little strange to be talking about guys when Lucy was missing, but I shook my head. "I kept thinking I should, but it seemed so obvious and forced. Like he'd know exactly why I was doing it."

"So?"

"That's not the way it's supposed to happen."

Courtney gave me an exasperated look. "According to whom?"

"I know, I know." We'd already discussed this at length. "According to my unrealistic notions about romance and guys and Sir Galahad and blah, blah, blah."

Courtney gave me an exaggerated nod, and said, "Yah-ha," which was her nice way of saying, "When are you going to snap out of your fantasy world and get it through your thick skull that guys just aren't the way you, Madison Archer, want them to be?"

"I know. I *know*."

"Well, maybe it's all for the best?" Courtney said. "Maybe

he's the wrong guy for you anyway? Like, I mean, you don't know anything about him. He just seemed to come out of nowhere."

"No," I countered. "He comes from some *place*. I just don't know where."

"Did you ask?"

"The opportunity didn't come up."

Courtney stared at me. "Wait a minute. Didn't you spend, like, half the night in the car with him?"

"Yes, I know. I just didn't . . . I don't know, I didn't feel comfortable prying. And I didn't want to seem too interested."

"You can ask where someone's from without sounding too interested, Madison."

I sighed. "I know."

"So how did it end?" she asked.

I told her about how he'd called Lucy a rich bitch and then saw where I lived and apologized and said he thought I was pretty nice.

"Yah-ha!" Courtney raised her eyebrows. "That's a hopeful sign."

"He only said it because he felt bad about the 'rich bitch' thing."

"Hello? You don't know that. Maybe he really thinks it. I mean, face it, Madison, you are *known* for being Miss Congeniality."

I was wondering how many Miss Congenialities wound up becoming Miss Old Maids when I turned into the driveway at Soundview High, an old three-story brick building with white columns in front. As we pulled into the student parking lot, I spotted Jen Waits on foot, dodging through the rows of parked cars to intercept us.

Jen was a short, busty cheerleader with blonde bangs, boundless energy, and an indefatigable zeal for being part of what she perceived to be "the right crowd." Impervious to slights and put-downs, she was a gossip of encyclopedic proportions.

"Brace yourself," Courtney muttered as I parked the Audi. Jen was motoring toward us fast enough to make her ample chest bounce under her tight sweater.

"You guys hear about Lucy?" she gasped, pink-cheeked from running. Before either of us could answer, she said, "Of course you have. But know what I heard? The police aren't doing anything! It's some weird policy they have for teenagers. They don't start to investigate unless you're gone for, like, a week. Because kids are always running away, you know?"

"Always?" I repeated doubtfully.

"That's what I heard. Anyway, I wonder how Adam is taking it. I mean, they did have a *huge* fight at the party." Jen gave Courtney a curious look. "Have you heard anything?"

I wondered why Jen had directed the question to Courtney.

"Since when am I the central clearing house for gossip?" Courtney asked pointedly.

"Just asking, okay?" Jen said with a shrug. "You were at the party. I saw you talking to him."

"So?" There was an uncharacteristic note of irritation in Courtney's voice.

"I just thought maybe you'd heard something," Jen said a bit sheepishly.

I was unaccustomed to seeing venom in Courtney's gaze, but there was no mistaking it now. I couldn't help wondering why.

In school the rumors were repeated. Lucy and Adam had had a big fight at the party. The police couldn't be bothered because too often teens disappeared for a day or two and then reappeared. But

I'd known Lucy since we were little kids. It was not like her to lose it just because she'd had a fight with her boyfriend. And run away? Lucy was the most competitive person I knew. That was the biggest reason why we'd ceased being close friends. It wasn't fun or even healthy to be friends with someone who always had to be better than you. Lucy Cunningham was the last person to run away from anything. But she was also bipolar and, therefore, unpredictable.

At lunch I picked at a salad while Courtney ravenously scarfed down several slices of truly unappetizing-looking cafeteria pizza. It seemed touchingly sad, given the Rajwars' affluence, that my friend had to depend on a school lunch to fill her nutritional needs.

"So . . . what was that about with Jen this morning?" I asked.

Courtney finished chewing and swallowed. "I was talking to Adam at the party and Lucy came over and just went off on him. It was totally innocent, but you know how she can get sometimes."

That was true. Lucy was possessive and territorial, and wouldn't hesitate to let Adam know when she thought he was getting too friendly with another girl. Across the cafeteria, Tyler emerged from the lunch line carrying a tray and wearing his trademark black leather trench coat. I watched as he scanned the tables, then headed for an empty one by the windows.

"The loner rebel," Courtney quipped.

"Maybe he's just shy," I said.

A wry smile appeared on her lips. "Whoever came up with the phrase 'Opposites attract' must have been thinking about you." She raised one eyebrow. "Why don't you go over?"

"And say what?"

"How about 'How are you?' or 'Nice weather we're having

today' or 'What do you think of them Yankees?'"

I laughed. "Their season ended a month ago. They didn't even make the playoffs."

Courtney rolled her eyes. "Whatever."

Tyler set his tray down on a table. Could I really go over and sit with him without seeming too pushy or just completely awkward? Why couldn't it just be something friendly to do? Was it because I knew I was interested in being more than just friends?

As Tyler sat down, he suddenly turned his head. Before I could look away, his eyes met mine. I froze, then forced a smile onto my lips. The smile Tyler responded with seemed sharp and knowing. Perhaps it was my imagination, but that smile seemed to say, *I know what you're thinking.*

"Busted," Courtney said.

I turned away, my face feeling hot.

"It's not the end of the world," she said. "It just means maybe you're interested."

"I feel so stupid."

"You know you're making way too much out of this. Like, look at it from his point of view? He's new at school, doesn't know anybody, sits alone at lunch every day. He's probably dying to become pals with someone like you who's near the red-hot center of the social universe. He'd be crazy not to."

"I don't think he cares. Not everyone does, you know."

Courtney waved her hand dismissively, as if anyone who didn't care didn't count. But it made me think of what PBleeker had written two nights before: *How come you only hang out with the popular clique?*

Courtney glanced at me and then her gaze rose over my shoulder. She stopped chewing, dabbed the corners of her mouth with a napkin, and smiled as widely as she could without parting her lips. It was the sort of self-conscious smile of someone worried that there might be something caught in her teeth. I wondered who she could be so concerned about her appearance for.

The answer came in the darkly ringed pale hazel eyes of Adam Pinter. He stopped beside Courtney, who swept some dark hair from her face and continued to give him that peculiar no-teeth smile. Adam's lips were pursed and the corners of his mouth turned down.

"Can we talk?" he asked me with unusual bluntness.

The question seemed to jar Courtney, as if it was the opposite of what she'd expected. At first she seemed startled, then a frown appeared. As I rose and followed Adam to an empty table, there was little doubt in my mind that there *was* something going on between Courtney and Adam, and I wondered why she had been reluctant to tell me.

We sat down. Adam leaned his elbows on the lunch table and interlocked his fingers. He was stocky and broad-shouldered with a five-o'clock shadow that usually began to show up around two. Now, with two days' worth of dark stubble covering his jaw, and his hair uncombed, he looked ragged and bleary.

"You were the last one to see Lucy," he said, gazing steadily at me. "Did she say anything?"

"Nothing that, you know, left any hint that she planned to do anything except go home."

Adam hung his head and ran his fingers through his hair. I'd known him for as long as I'd known Lucy, and in many ways we'd been closer friends, something that had always bothered Lucy. Adam, she, and I had been in school together since kindergarten, but Lucy's relentless competitiveness had always made her harder to trust. You could never be certain that she wouldn't betray you if it meant winning something she wanted. Adam and I had always felt more naturally comfortable and easy together. We'd shared secrets.

"Why would she run away? Where would she go? It doesn't make sense." The questions were rhetorical. No one was in a better position to answer them than Adam himself.

"Is it true that about the police, not looking for her right away?"

Adam shrugged. "They *say* that's their policy if there's no evidence of foul play." He lowered his voice. "They don't want every parent in town demanding a full investigation every time a kid decides to sleep at his girlfriend's house and doesn't call home. But the Cunninghams told the cops about the bipolar stuff and that all Lucy had on her was her cell phone and keys. No ID. She'd left her wallet home that night. No money or credit cards. No medications. Just the clothes she was wearing." The anguish in his voice was palpable.

I reached across the table and placed my hand over his. Adam blinked hard and looked away. After a moment he turned back. His eyes were watery and red-rimmed. I could not remember the last time I'd seen him with tears in his eyes. Certainly never after second grade.

"Maybe there was something she said," he almost pleaded. "Something that sounded totally innocent at the time."

"There wasn't, Adam," I said. "I wish I could say there was, but I've thought really hard about it, and there isn't."

Adam pressed his lips into a hard, flat line. "I feel awful for her parents. This is the kind of thing they've probably been afraid of for years."

"She could still turn up at any moment," I said. "For all we know, she just showed up at her front door." I squeezed his hand reassuringly.

At the same time, I glanced out of the corner of my eye at Courtney, a few tables away, watching us. When our eyes met, she quickly looked away. I turned back to Adam. "I heard there were some guys from FCC at the party?"

Fairchester Community College wasn't a place many kids from Soundview went to, unless they couldn't get into a four-year school. The lines between Adam's eyes wrinkled. "Yeah, but . . . I don't think Lucy said a word to them. We were pretty much in sight of each other the whole night . . . I mean, until the argument."

I kept my hand firmly on his. Strangely, Adam was the one boy my age I felt completely comfortable with physically. Maybe because we'd always been friends and nothing more. "If I can do anything . . ."

Adam nodded. "Thanks, Mads, I appreciate it."

Mads was his private nickname for me. I glanced again at Courtney. She was staring at my hand on Adam's, a look of dismay on her face.

* * *

37

Str-S-d #7

At school today everyone was talking about how Lucy Cunningham has disappeared. Some people think Lucy ran away and some people think she was kidnapped. I just think, who cares? Good riddance. It's a relief to walk down the hall without seeing her look at me like I don't deserve to live. God, I hate her. I'm glad she's gone and I hope she never comes back.

∙∙

💬 **4 Comments**

Realgurl4013 said...
Luuucky you! I wish I could make some of the kids around heeere disappeeear.

IaMnEmEsIs said...
People get what they deserve.

Tony2theman said...
Why be sorry? She sounds like a real bee-ach.

ApRilzDay said...
Don't you feel a little weird? I mean, isn't it kind of like your wish really came true?

chapter 5

Tuesday 7:05 A.M.

THE AIR WAS clear and chilly. Val's and my breaths came out in plumes of white vapor. She was frisky this morning and I sensed that she wanted to canter, but I kept her at a trot because I wanted to think without worrying about where we were going. It was Tuesday, and Lucy was still gone.

The trees were bare, but the ground still had splotches of orange, red, and yellow. As Val trotted down the wooded path, I heard the crunch and clatter of a deer crashing away through the underbrush. It was no use trying to imagine where Lucy was. The night before there'd been rumors and IMs speculating on an impulsive rendezvous with an old camp friend, a chance meeting with an L.A. talent agent, an impulsive fling with one of the guys from FCC who'd been at the party. All were possible. But then again, the impossible never became rumor, did it?

I turned my thoughts to Tyler. Ever since grade school I'd made it a practice every six months to develop a crush on some mysterious boy with whom my path had crossed at a sports field or on vacation somewhere, or in the waiting room at my orthodontist. Usually these mystery crushes were brief and unfulfilled, as I never had the nerve, or guile, to make contact. But with Tyler it was different. He was at school day after day, so there were opportunities aplenty. It was actually hard to come up with excuses for *not* trying to connect with him. Besides, I kept reminding myself, I was a senior and had never had a real, steady boyfriend. It was my goal to have one by the time I graduated.

The alarm on my cell phone chimed. It was time to turn Val around and head back to the stable, and from there, to school.

When playwrights, novelists, and songwriters wanted to pick a town for their characters to either dream of living in, or to hold up as an example of all that was too materialistic and trendy and chic, they often chose Soundview. Almost everybody who lived here was well-to-do, if not just plain rich. Many drove fancy European cars, had vacation homes at faraway beaches or ski areas, and took several long holidays a year. It was said that Soundviewers exuded an air of entitlement—they felt they deserved the best of everything.

Back in the 1990s, a group of parents, worried that their kids might take "the entitled life" for granted, got together and urged the high school to institute a mandatory community-service requirement. Among the programs kids could choose from were Habitat for Humanity, Meals on Wheels, or Safe Rides. That fall Courtney had signed up for Safe Rides mostly because I had.

"Can you believe Ms. Skelling is calling an emergency *lunch* meeting?" she asked irritably on the lunch line. Everyone in Safe Rides had gotten e-mails the night before from our faculty advisor. I'd actually been glad, since it would mean seeing Tyler.

"Why can't it wait?" Courtney went on. "We usually meet on Thursdays. She is such a pain. I wish I'd signed up for Meals on Wheels, except old people creep me out."

"I guess we'll see pretty soon," I said, wondering what was really bothering her. "So . . . still no news about Lucy."

Courtney slid her tray down the rail and said nothing. One of my faults, I'd been told, was that because I hated confrontations. I always went out of my way to be nice and undemanding. And that sometimes worked against me because some people thought they could step all over me. So I was trying to be more assertive.

"I thought we told each other everything," I said.

"I don't know what you're talking about." Courtney kept her eyes averted.

"Lucy . . . and you and Adam."

"Why ask me?" my friend said.

"Because yesterday morning Jen seemed to think there was something going on between you two, and because I saw the way you looked at Adam at lunch yesterday."

Courtney reached for a steaming bowl filled with the most unappetizing spaghetti and meatballs I had ever seen. "I think you're imagining things, okay?"

I thought I wasn't, but I also sensed that this wasn't the time to push the topic harder. We were supposed to eat quickly and then head for the science lab, the regular Safe Rides meeting place, because Ms. Skelling taught chemistry. I picked at my salad while Courtney hungrily gobbled down the spaghetti and meatballs, then we headed toward the cafeteria exit.

Out in the hall we passed my homeroom teacher, Mrs. Towner.

She was a tiny woman, not even five feet tall, and was very pregnant. She was walking slowly, with one hand on her swollen belly and the other on her hip. I gave her a friendly wave and she smiled weakly.

"Women are *so* not meant to be pregnant," Courtney whispered with a wink.

As we passed the girls' room I stopped. "Go ahead. I'll catch up."

Courtney scowled. "It really ticks Ms. Skelling off when we're late."

"I'll just be a second. Go ahead."

The scowl became a knowing smile. "Yah-ha! Let's look nice for Tyler?"

"Don't be so smart," I said, and went in. At the mirror I touched up my hair and makeup. It felt wrong to be thinking about my looks and Tyler when Lucy was missing, but there was still no reason to believe that anything bad had happened. There had to be lots of innocent explanations for her disappearance, even if we couldn't think of them.

I'd only meant to be a second in the girls' room, but I guess I dawdled because when I got to the Safe Rides meeting everyone was already seated on stools at the lab tables.

"Why Madison, we're so glad you could take time from your busy schedule to join us," Ms. Skelling said with her unique way of gilding sarcasm with gentility. The Safe Rides advisor affected a slightly regal demeanor that some kids thought was obnoxious. She frequently hinted that she came from a well-to-do family in the area known as the Main Line outside Philadelphia.

"Sorry, everyone," I said. Just about every stool was taken, except for one next to Tyler. It was almost a dream come true. I sat down next to him and he gave me a slight nod.

Ms. Skelling was a tall, broad-shouldered woman with bright, dyed red hair. She was new at our school that year and tended to wear too much mascara and eye shadow, favored copious amounts of vintage costume jewelry, and preferred name-brand outfits from Chanel, Dior, and Cardin that, given her teacher's salary, I had to believe came from thrift shops. She often wore her blouses with one extra button open, revealing crevice-like cleavage, which the boys craned their necks to enjoy and, some girls suspected, was not of entirely natural origins.

"We were just talking about Lucy Cunningham," she said. "You're part of that crowd, Madison. What have you heard?"

There it was again—the same thing PBleeker had said. Maybe, if I *was* part of "that crowd," it was because they were the only ones who invited me to do things with them.

I shook my head. "The same rumors everyone else has heard."

"Someone said the police aren't investigating," said Dave Ignatzia, a slightly built guy who wore thick glasses and whose dark hair fell down on his forehead. "They don't consider you a missing person unless you've been gone at least a week. What if she's been kidnapped? By the time a week passes, it could be too late."

"Dude, if she's been kidnapped, someone'll get in touch with her parents asking for ransom," Tyler said.

"Unless they didn't kidnap her for money," Courtney pointed out.

"You mean, like they're holding her as a sex prisoner?" Behind the thick glasses, Dave's eyes went wide.

"Easy, Dave, keep your pants on," said Sharon Costello, the squat, broad-shouldered half of an inseparable duo. Seated beside her was Laurie Clark, a tall, quiet girl who often came to school with greasy, unwashed hair.

"Screw you," Dave stammered.

"You wish," Sharon baited him.

"With you? No way," Dave shot back. "I'd rather stay a . . ." He trailed off, but it was too late. Sharon pounced.

"A virgin?" she cackled. "Is that what you were going to say?"

Dave's face turned red. "No."

"Yes, it was!" Sharon insisted gleefully.

"S-so? Look who's talking," Dave sputtered. "You're probably a virgin for life."

"Only in your narrow definition of the word," Sharon shot back, resting her hand on Laurie's forearm.

I glanced at Ms. Skelling, who normally didn't tolerate such banter in her presence, but the chemistry teacher was staring out the window, almost as if she were in a daze.

"Isn't a week a long time?" asked shy, mousy Maura Bresliss in barely more than a whisper.

The sound of her voice seemed to bring Ms. Skelling back to the room. She turned her gaze on Tyler and me. "You're both aware that you're supposed to stay until the client enters the house. Please tell me why standard operating procedure wasn't followed?"

It caught me by surprise when Tyler had cocked his eyebrow at me as if to let everyone know that it was my responsibility to answer. For a moment I felt a twinge of resentment, but then I told myself that perhaps he was right. After all, I *had* been the one who'd urged him to leave Lucy standing there in the dark.

I could have said that Lucy was being a total jerk, but that wasn't the point. Jerk or not, we were supposed to wait. That's why they called it Safe Rides and not just Rides.

"It was late and I was tired," I said. "I didn't think—"

"Obviously," Ms. Skelling interjected. "Or, more precisely, you *did* think . . . but only about yourself. Really, Madison, what is the first thing you learned about people who've been drinking? They can't be expected to make responsible decisions. That's what *you're* supposed to do for them. If Lucy didn't get to her house, it's probably because she made an irresponsible decision to go somewhere else."

"Or someone abducted her," Dave reminded everyone.

"Nobody abducted her," Courtney said irritably.

"How do you know?"

"Because this is *Soundview*, Dave." Courtney may have sounded just a little bit haughty, but she actually reflected the way most of us felt. Our parents had moved here for the excellent schools, and because it was safe and secure. The worst crimes were usually DWIs and, now and then, a break in.

Besides, to kidnap or abduct someone, you had to know where they'd be so you could lie in wait for them. Lucy's call to Safe Rides didn't come in until after two thirty. The only people who could have known where she was going were a few at the party.

And the people in this room . . .

But before I had time to think about that, Ms. Skelling turned on me again. "I think it's important for you to understand the gravity of what you've done, Madison. You know I don't like to single people out, but honestly, you've jeopardized the whole purpose of this group. Who's going to call a service that lost someone? And why are we in this spot? Because you, my dear, selfishly put your need for sleep ahead of someone else's safety."

I wasn't sure what hurt more, the harshness of her criticism or the fact that no one in the group came to my defense. In particular, I felt let down by Tyler, who was—at least in some part—responsible, too.

The meeting ended. Usually I left with Courtney, but she popped up and exited the room before I had a chance to join her. Instead, I found myself leaving the lab at the same time as Tyler. Walking beside him in the noisy, crowded hall, I had mixed feelings. Part of me hoped we might pick up where we'd left off early Sunday morning, when he'd said he thought I was pretty nice. But another part was still feeling humiliated by what Ms. Skelling had just said. Meanwhile Tyler hardly looked at me as we walked down the hall.

"Listen, this isn't an excuse," I said, "but I have to believe that we're not the first crew who ever left someone before they got into their house."

Tyler glanced briefly at me and kept walking. Part of me wanted to turn away in another direction, but another part of me yearned to hear him reply. Besides, I couldn't quite believe he'd be so rude that he wouldn't answer.

Just when I concluded that he was ignoring me, he suddenly stopped and turned to me. Why did I find his gaze so unsettling? Was it his dark hair and eyes? His confidence? I felt goose bumps rise on my skin, and a singular thought burst into my head. I didn't want him to talk. I wanted him to scoop me into his arms and kiss me. Right there in the hall. In front of everyone. I didn't care. I wanted to feel his arms around me. I wanted to be enveloped in his intensity.

Instead he said, "Things like this happen for a reason."

It felt like I'd been in a hot shower that had suddenly turned freezing cold. "What does that mean?"

"Just what I said."

I stared at him, not comprehending. Maybe I wasn't able to comprehend because part of me was still in that fantasy where he took me in his arms. Tyler frowned and then continued on, leaving me staring, perplexed, at the back of his long black coat.

Tuesday 4:43 P.M.

Poor Lucy, look at you, shivering and dirty. Thirsty, you say? Yes, we imagine you would be. Feels terrible, doesn't it? You'd give anything for a drink of cool clear water right now, wouldn't you? Just think of that fresh water. Imagine how good it will feel going down your parched throat. Yes, we have it right here. All the water you can drink. All you have to do is beg. Sorry? Is this degrading? Really? But just think of how degraded you've made others feel. Never thought about that, did you? All the pain and misery you caused. You say you realize it now? We're proud of you, Lucy. What? The water? Did we really say you could have all the water you wanted? Silly us. Sorry, you're not getting any.

* * *

"WHAT DO YOU want to do on Thursday?" Sharon asked Laurie as they walked home after field-hockey practice on Tuesday afternoon. The day had started sunny but turned gray and cold. Both girls wore sweats and hoodies with their hands jammed into the pockets.

"I don't know," Laurie answered.

No surprise, Sharon thought. Laurie never knew what she wanted to do. She never made suggestions, or had a plan. She was like clay, willing to be molded into anything you wanted.

"Well, what do you *think* you want to do?" Sharon asked.

"I don't know."

Sharon sighed irritably. Could anyone really be such a total blank? "Do you want to go to the movies? Or the mall? Or stay home and watch TV?"

"Any of them is fine," Laurie answered with a smile.

"I think we should go to the movies," Sharon said. "And let's go out to eat first. What do you want to eat?"

"I don't care."

"Pizza or Chinese?"

"You decide."

"Why can't *you* ever decide?"

"I don't know. You're the one who always likes to decide."

"Just for once, I want you to decide."

"But I don't care."

"How can you not care?" Sharon asked.

"I just don't, okay? It's not that important to me. It seems way more important to you, so you decide."

Sharon wanted to scream . . . or hit her. Why, of all the girls in the world, had she gotten stuck with such a wuss? Why couldn't she have met someone . . . *anyone* else? But that was the problem with a place like Soundview. There were just the two of them. And if there was anyone else, she was either in deep denial or deep in the closet. So for now Sharon was stuck with this one. But not for much longer. She was counting the days. As soon as high school was over, she was off to San Francisco and a whole new life.

"Okay," she said, "pizza and then the movies."

"Fine," said Laurie.

"There's that new Claw movie," Sharon said. "It's supposed to be really scary."

"Okay."

"But there's also that comedy? The one about the guy who has to hide out in the all-girl school?"

"Sounds good."

"So which one do you want to see?"

"Either one."

"Don't you ever have an opinion about anything?" Sharon asked, exasperated.

"I don't know. Sometimes. What's the big deal, Sharon?"

"Okay, I just decided I don't want pizza and a movie," Sharon said. "I want McDonald's and then we'll go to the billiard place and play Eight Ball."

"All right."

Sharon stopped and faced her girlfriend. "No, I just changed my mind again. That's not what I want to do. What I really want to do this Thursday is kill someone."

Laurie just stared at her. There was no expression on her face.

chapter 7

Tuesday 6:51 P.M.

MOM AND I had salads for dinner. Dad was out of town on business. We were used to eating without him, but tonight, because of what had happened to Lucy, it felt lonely and isolated in our big house at the end of the point.

Mom probably felt the same way I did, but she could always be counted on for a brave smile. "God, I feel for the Cunninghams," she said. "Paul and Dana are utterly beside themselves." Through the kitchen window we watched a cloud of white terns wheel and dive over a school of splashing fish in the Sound. "It's been three days. I think I'd go mad if I were them. What's it like at school?"

"Weird," I said. "Everyone's tronning."

"Sorry?"

"Pretending things are normal, even though we know they're not. Ms. Skelling really dumped on me today for leaving Lucy before she went into the house."

Mom's forehead wrinkled. "That's not right."

I pushed at a slice of cucumber with my fork, feeling a wretched mixture of guilt and regret and fright. "No, she was right. I either should have gotten her to go inside or waited."

"You said Lucy didn't want to go in," Mom said. "Were you supposed to sit there and wait all night until she did?"

I shrugged and felt my eyes become watery. The emotions I'd held down all day had finally begun to overflow. I always tried to do the right thing. My mother was my model. She was always involved in one cause or another. After one career on the school board, and another as the Mayor of Soundview, she now ran the Archer Foundation, the charitable part of my dad's company that gave money, usually anonymously, to good causes. As a result, she, too, had to travel, but not as often. She also worked with local civic organizations, like the PTO and the library. I'd been brought up with the understanding that I'd do the same sort of things. In the summer I gave time to Habitat for Humanity, and in the winter I probably would have done Safe Rides even if I hadn't been required to.

The tears spilled out and ran down my cheeks. Mom slid her chair close to mine and hugged me. "It's not your fault, hon. There's no way you could have known. You wouldn't have even been there if you hadn't been trying to help."

"Doesn't matter." I sniffed and rubbed the tears out of my eyes.

"It *does* matter," Mom insisted. "Things happen. You can't control them. You can only do the best you can."

"I could have made sure she got inside. That would have been the best."

Mom squeezed me in her arms. "You had no reason to. Nothing like this has ever happened around here before, and you said Lucy was being difficult. There's no way you or anyone else could have known."

I blew my nose and rested my head against her shoulder. "I'm scared, Mom."

"Why?" she asked, sounding surprised.

"I don't know. I guess because nothing like this has ever happened here before. . . . What if something awful's happened to Lucy?"

"We don't know," Mom said, and hugged me. "There's no point in getting upset until—"

"Until we *know* something bad's happened?" I finished the sentence for her.

"That's not what I meant to say."

"But it's what you were thinking."

Mom's lips parted as if to argue, but then she nodded. "Yes, you're right. It's hard not to imagine that something bad has happened. But we can't give up hope."

Leaving most of the salad on the plate, I went upstairs after dinner. As soon as I turned on the computer, a message from PBleeker was there.

This thing with Lucy is freaky, isn't it? I wish I could talk to you about it. Just call you up like a friend and share thoughts. You'd probably be nice and polite for a couple of minutes and then make some excuse to get off the phone. Because you've got tons of more important friends to talk to. I can't understand why someone like you doesn't have a boyfriend. Unless he goes to a different school. Or he's in college. That would make sense. You wouldn't give anyone around here a chance.

Why pick on me? I wondered. There were other girls who were prettier and more popular (at least they *cared* about popularity more than I did). Why couldn't PBleeker send those creepy messages to one of them? I deleted the message and turned on some music. But it didn't matter. PBleeker was still there, in the air, in my mind, out in the dark. Lucy was gone and my cyberstalker was there. And for the first time in my life, Soundview didn't feel like a safe place at all.

Str-S-d #8

It's been three days since Lucy Cunningham disappeared. I know I said good riddance and everything, but it is a little strange. I mean, no one from around here has ever just vanished before. Wait a minute, why should I care? Would Lucy care if I disappeared? Not a chance. She'd be so relieved not to have to look at me. She wouldn't even give me a second thought. I take back what I just said. I don't care what happened to her. I'm glad that she's gone.

....

💬 6 Comments

ApRilzDay said...

It sounds like something you're trying to convince yourself of. Like you don't really believe you're that cold and uncaring. Aren't you worried that if you stop caring you'll just become hollow and bitter? Maybe Lucy deserved to be knocked down a few pegs. But did she really deserve to disappear? If she's been gone three days, something bad really might have happened!

Str-S-d said...

You don't know how it feels to be tormented.

IaMnEmEsIs said...

There is justice in tormenting the tormentor.

Realgurl4013 said...

I sooo agreee.

Tony2theman said...

Sounds like that Lucy chick could be pushin' up daisies.

IaMnEmEsIs said...

Soon.

Wednesday 6:42 A.M.

"WE JUST WANT Lucy back unharmed." The familiar voice came from the kitchen the next morning. It was Dr. Cunningham. *Why is he in our kitchen?* I wondered as I trudged through the doorway, still half asleep. But inside I saw that it was only his face on the TV.

Mom was sitting at the kitchen counter with a mug of coffee, watching. On the TV, Lucy's dad, usually meticulously neat and groomed, looked haggard and unshaven with bags under his eyes. "If you have information that will help us get our daughter, Lucy, back, we will pay one hundred thousand dollars, no questions asked. If you are the person who has Lucy, I urge you to get in touch and tell us what you want. We are willing to negotiate. Lucy, if you're watching this, we love you and will do everything in our power to get you home again."

"Those poor, poor people." Mom's words were heavy with angst. "Your heart absolutely goes out to them."

Outside, rain poured down from the gray sky. The Sound was choppy, and a pair of gulls hovered in the wind. The TV screen cut to the local morning news anchor with a photograph of Lucy behind him. "It's been four days since seventeen-year-old

Lucy Cunningham of Soundview disappeared without a trace. Police admit they have no leads. As you just saw, the Cunningham family is offering a one-hundred-thousand-dollar reward for information leading to her safe return."

The scene switched to the outside of the Soundview police station, where a reporter wearing a red rain slicker and holding a microphone said, "Police here in Soundview say the investigation is ongoing. Ms. Cunningham is the daughter of a well-known cardiologist, and people close to the investigation say kidnapping is a possibility, but so far no one has demanded a ransom."

The screen cut back to the news anchor and his blonde co-anchor. "Sounds like this is a situation where you almost hope she *has* been kidnapped."

The blonde co-anchor nodded in agreement. "You mean, because that's the lesser of several evils?"

"Exactly," the anchor said with a pensive nod, and then turned to the camera again. "In other news . . ."

My stomach began to hurt. Ever since I'd been little, I'd gotten stomachaches whenever I felt anxious or worried. I could feel one coming, and crossed my arms over my stomach and bent forward.

Mom reached forward and brushed some hairs off my forehead. She gave me a searching, concerned look. "Maybe you should stay home today."

The suggestion surprised me. Usually, when I got a stomachache, Mom encouraged me to tough it out. "But—" I said.

"I know it doesn't make complete sense, but I'd just as soon you stayed home," Mom said patiently. "I don't think it will hurt you to miss one day."

"You're . . . worried?"

She nodded. "It looks like they think it might be a kidnapping. I know they aren't sure—and that it's extremely unlikely that, if it is a kidnapping, the kidnappers would strike again in the same place. But I think there are times when you can't be too careful. Times when it's best to err on the side of caution. I'm sure your father would feel the same way."

We agreed that I'd skip school. Later, Mom left for a meeting in the city and I went upstairs and slept for another hour. When I woke, my stomachache had vanished. I did some schoolwork and fooled around on the computer for a while, but something in my head was nagging me to go back downstairs.

In the kitchen I made a mug of peppermint tea and turned on the TV. The local channel repeated the morning show half a dozen times during the day, and it wasn't long before I was once again watching the segment with Lucy's dad offering the reward for her safe return. As Mom had said, kidnapping was a possibility. It seemed so crazy and unreal. These kinds of things just didn't happen here.

I sipped the tea and turned the TV off. My thoughts wandered, and whenever that happened lately, Tyler was waiting nearby. Why, the day before, had he said that everything happens for a reason? Was he just trying to appear cool and mysterious? And that reminded me of how Ms. Skelling had ripped into me about leaving Lucy on the street outside her house. What a mean thing to do. Did she think I didn't already feel bad enough without having to make me feel worse? And that made me think of

Courtney, who'd popped up so quickly from her seat after the meeting and vanished into the hall before I could find her. Why had she done that? Did it have something to do with Adam? Why did I feel like everyone had secrets? Was that true, or was I just being paranoid?

I looked up at the clock. At school, fifth period would be ending in a few moments. Courtney would be going to study hall, a class she could always be late for. I sent her a text: *?4U*

Normally, she would hit me right back.

I waited.

No reply.

On any other day I might have assumed the message hadn't gone through, or maybe her phone had died. But today I had to wonder. Was she ignoring me?

I sent a second text: *PTM*. Please text me.

But she didn't.

I finished the tea and felt a weird combination of anxiety and boredom. I'd told Mom I wouldn't go to school, but I hadn't said I wouldn't leave the house. Besides, it was day, not the middle of the night when bad things happened. Even Mom had said that it was highly unlikely that kidnappers would strike twice. And it seemed even more unlikely that they'd do it in the middle of the day.

School would be ending soon. By now Courtney had had plenty of time to answer my texts. I could only assume that she was ignoring me. But she was supposed to be my closest friend. If that was no longer the case, I wanted to know.

I got dressed and went out. The air was cold and damp and there were puddles in the driveway, but at least it had stopped raining. It was hard to know where Courtney would go after school. Sometimes she went into town and hung out at the Starbucks. Sometimes she went to the mall, or to one of her other friend's houses. Most of the time she didn't go home until dinner.

After deciding that the best place to find her after dismissal would be near school, I drove over and parked a few blocks away. Pulling my hoodie tight around my head, I stood at the bus stop. It wasn't long before the front doors opened and kids began flooding out.

Courtney came out alone, her red backpack slung over one shoulder, her long black hair with those streaks of pink and blonde dancing. Since she was alone, I assumed she wasn't going to a friend's house. That was good news, because it meant she would pass me on the way to town or the mall.

But instead of making a right at the bottom of the steps, she made a left. That was bad news, because to catch up to her I'd have to walk right past school.

Hoping that no one would recognize me, I started down the sidewalk. Courtney was walking fast, which was totally not like her. I wondered if she was going to meet someone. Rather than rush to catch up, I hung back and decided to see.

She turned right on the next block, entering the residential neighborhood closest to the school. This was one of the older neighborhoods in town, and not many kids we knew lived there. Where was she going? At the next corner she turned left. By now it was just me and her on the sidewalk.

As she walked, she took out a compact and checked her makeup. Now I was certain she was meeting someone. It was all so strange to me. I thought I knew almost everything about her. Could she really have a secret life I knew nothing about?

At the next corner she turned right and started to speed up. I practically had to jog to keep her in sight. Then she looked back at me and started to run.

I started to run after her. Every twenty feet she would look back at me. Suddenly I realized what was happening. She knew someone was following her, but with my hoodie on, she didn't know who it was. I pulled the hood back and called, "Courts, wait! It's me, Madison!"

Courtney looked back and stopped. She bent over and placed her hands on her thighs. As I got closer, I could see that she was panting for breath. "You scared . . . *the crap* out of me."

"I didn't mean to."

"What . . . are you doing? Why . . . were you following me?"

"I came to school to find out why you weren't answering my texts."

Courtney kept panting. "Why weren't . . . you in school today?"

"Mom saw Lucy's dad on TV this morning offering a reward for her return. It freaked her out. I mean, the whole idea that Lucy might have been kidnapped. She wanted me to stay home."

Courtney nodded and straightened up. She breathed deeply and ran her fingers through her long black hair.

"Who were you going to meet?" I asked.

"No one."

"A few moments ago you were checking your makeup in your mirror," I said.

"A few moments ago I was looking in my mirror to figure out who was following me. For God's sake, Madison, you totally scared the crap out of me."

"Yes, you already told me that."

We stared at each other. It felt like we'd reached a stalemate. "Are you going to tell me what's going on or not?" I asked.

Courtney looked around. "How'd you get here?"

"My car. It's parked back on Rosewood."

"Give me a ride to Starbucks?" she asked.

"Aren't you going somewhere?"

"I just want some coffee."

"When did it start?" I asked twenty minutes later as we sat at a small table inside Starbucks. Courtney had just admitted to me that she'd been seeing Adam on the down low. Based on the way she'd been acting, I should have guessed, but I hadn't. In fact, I was totally blown away. Courtney propped her elbows on the table and cupped the double latte I'd bought her in both hands, as if using it to warm them.

"Junior prom."

I stared at her in astonishment. *"Last year?"*

"Shhhhh!" She hushed me and her eyes darted left and right at the other kids sitting around tables and at the counter. "It's been on and off."

"But why?"

"Why has it been on and off? Or why did I do it?"

"The latter."

Courtney raised and dropped her shoulders. "He's a studmuffin."

As if it was that simple. As if Adam wasn't Lucy's boyfriend. As if this wasn't about the most scandalous thing I'd ever known her to do.

"There are lots of other muffins," I said. "I think you'll have to do better than that."

She rolled her eyes dramatically. "Why do you care?"

"For one thing, I thought we were friends. I thought we told each other everything."

Courtney sipped the latte and licked some foam off her upper lip. "You used to be best friends with Lucy."

Now I understood. "You thought I'd tell her?"

"I don't know. You're also friends with Adam. It was complicated. And he doesn't want anyone to know, either."

"If he likes you, why didn't he just break up with her?"

"He was going to. I think that's what that fight on Saturday night was about. But you know Lucy. It wasn't like she'd just let him dump her without making a huge stink."

Then there was indeed a reason why Lucy might have decided to run away, or do something else that people would think of as extreme. "Do the Cunninghams know that it wasn't just a fight? That Adam was planning to actually break up with Lucy?"

Courtney frowned. "How would I know?"

Suddenly I realized something. "I have to talk to Adam."

"Why?"

"Because Lucy is the most competitive person I know. Adam breaking up with her is exactly the kind of thing that could make her snap. The Cunninghams have to be told about this."

"Do they have to know that I was involved?" Courtney asked.

I thought for a moment. "No. I don't think so." I started to get up.

"Where are you going?" Courtney asked.

"I told you. I have to speak to Adam."

"So call him."

"No, Courts, this is something I have to do in person. Come on, I'll give you a ride home."

She heaved a big sigh, as if she thought I was making more out of it than necessary. But I was certain she was wrong.

"So," I said a few moments later in the car. "Back to my original question. Why Adam?"

Courtney gazed out the side window and didn't answer. I had a feeling she was fed up with me. If my intention back at Starbucks had been to patch things up, I'd done a really bad job. Now I wasn't sure what I wanted. I just knew I didn't want to leave everything unresolved. We were getting close to her house, and I pulled off to the side of the road.

"What are you doing?" Courtney asked, sounding very annoyed.

"Waiting for an answer."

"I thought you were in a big rush to go see Adam."

"Is it really going to take that long to tell me?"

Once again Courtney rolled her eyes as if I'd just taken her to a new height in exasperation. "What is your problem?"

"Look, I can understand why you didn't want to tell me about Adam before. But now that I know, why can't you say why? I mean, if you were just looking to hook up, there are plenty of other *studmuffins* you could have chosen."

Courtney stared at me. "Ohmygod! Are you jealous?"

"No. I'm just . . . I don't know. Maybe I feel protective of him. We've been friends for so long."

"You don't *own* him."

"I think I'm aware of that," I said. "And he and you and every-one else is free to do whatever they want. But seriously, Courts? Why Adam?"

My friend rapped her deep-purple nails against the Star-bucks cup that she'd brought into the car with her. Suddenly she reached for the door handle and yanked. The next thing I knew, she grabbed her bag from the back and got out. "Thanks for the ride and the coffee. I can walk the rest of the way from here."

chapter 9

Wednesday 3:31 P.M.

Oh, dear, Lucy, look at you, huddled in the corner with your arms around your knees. You are looking awfully gaunt and dirty. You do look thinner. It's so sad. Lack of water and food will wreck havoc on your beautiful figure. Oh, Lucy, just imagine yourself without your perfect figure. What a tragedy it would be to look just like the rest of us.

Are you shivering? Well, it has gotten colder, hasn't it? And all this rain. What's this? Look at your arms and legs. Scratching yourself until you're bloody? How odd. Was that something your medications were supposed to prevent? Or are you just trying to show us that you're repenting? Repent all you want, my dear. We're sorry, but it won't bring you salvation.

* * *

ONE DAY WHEN Adam and I were seven, we played doctor. Ever since then, we'd teased each other about whose idea it had been, each of us claiming we'd been talked into it by the other. But the truth, at least as I recalled, was that we'd both been willing participants. And it was a secret we'd never shared with anyone else.

I don't know if that was what helped me feel comfortable with him, but he was always more like a brother or a cousin to me. Someone I knew I could trust and depend on to do the right thing.

The Pinters lived in a large old house with a brook running behind it. Even though it was cold and damp from the earlier rain, Adam's younger brothers were out in the driveway playing basketball. They paused and briefly stared at me when I parked down the driveway. Then they went back to playing ball. They seemed used to girls coming by to see their older brother.

I went up to the front door and rang the bell. A few moments later I heard Mrs. Pinter cautiously ask, "Who's there?"

"Hi, Mrs. Pinter, it's Madison."

The door opened. Given the size of her sons, Mrs. Pinter was a surprisingly small person with dark hair coiffed in a slightly old-fashioned way. She smiled. "Madison, what a surprise. How are you?"

I shrugged and forced something that was supposed to resemble cheer on my face. "I don't know. Okay, I guess."

"I understand," Adam's mom said, her smile fading. "He's in his room."

I took the stairs up. A large, bright yellow YIELD sign hung on Adam's door. I knocked.

"Yeah?"

"It's Madison."

A chair creaked. Adam came to the door wearing jeans, a hoodie, and a scowl. His eyes were still puffy and darkly ringed. "Were you at school today?"

"Took a mental-health day." I lowered my voice. "I have to talk to you about something, and I didn't feel comfortable doing it over the phone."

Adam opened the door wider and stepped back, allowing me in. On the floor, along with the weights, was a pile of SAT-prep manuals. I sat down on the bed. "Courtney told me about you and her, and that you were planning on breaking up with Lucy. Do the Cunninghams know?"

Adam's eyes widened with astonishment. Then he hung his head. "Yeah. I didn't want to tell them, but I had to."

"Then she *could* have snapped. She could have run away or . . . I mean, we really don't know what she'd do."

"You really believe that, Mads?"

"I'm just saying it's possible. No one can absolutely know."

Adam turned toward his computer screen. "I can't say for certain that she isn't capable of doing something to herself. But I'm pretty sure she wouldn't do it because of me." He paused and moved the cursor. "You know, I wasn't really her boyfriend, Mads. I was just another trophy. Another achievement in the personal résumé she kept in her head. Sometimes I think she had to have me mostly because she couldn't deal with the idea of me being anyone else's boyfriend."

I knew Lucy well enough to know that could have been true.

"On TV this morning Dr. Cunningham sounded like he thought she'd been kidnapped."

Adam winced. "Maybe because it's better than the alternative, you know? It's been what? Four days? Four days without her medications? Without any money? Four days and no one's seen any sign of her? You really have to hope she's with someone somewhere, because if she isn't . . ." Adam didn't finish the sentence. He just shook his head.

"But who could she be with?" I asked.

Adam didn't answer. He didn't have to.

On my way home, I pulled up to the gate at the entrance to Premium Point and waved inside to the guard. He raised a finger, as if motioning me to wait, then slid the window open and held something out. "Someone left this for you."

It was a plain white paper napkin, folded over until it was the size of a Post-it. *Madison Archer* was written on it in thick, smudged pencil. I unfolded it.

YOU AND YOUR FRIENDS ARE IN DANGER.
I CAN TELL YOU MORE, BUT FIRST I
HAVE TO KNOW THAT I CAN TRUST YOU.

My whole body grew tense and my stomach started to knot. "Where did you get this?"

"It was wedged into the doorframe when I came on duty." The guard narrowed one eye quizzically. "You okay, Miss Archer?"

"Yes, thank you."

Back in my room I read it again. *First I have to know that I can trust you.* What did that mean? That I wasn't to tell the police? But how would the writer know if I did or didn't? How did I even know if this was real and not some kind of a joke?

I was pondering these questions when the garage door opened. Mom was home.

Half an hour later, Detective Payne of the Soundview Police Department was sitting at our kitchen table, sipping a cup of coffee. The detective was a thin man with a blond moustache. The note lay open on the kitchen table.

"Do you think it's real?" Mom asked.

Detective Payne made a gesture with his hands to show he didn't know. "It's like anything else these days. We have to treat it as legitimate until we know otherwise." He turned to me. "Why do you think this note came to you, Madison?"

I shook my head. "I don't have a clue."

"Can you think of anyone who might want to play with your head?" the detective asked.

PBleeker, I thought. "There might be one person. I'm not sure. I get anonymous messages."

Mom wrinkled her forehead. "How long has this been going on?"

"About a year."

"Why didn't you tell us?"

"Because I never really felt threatened. It's more like some-one who, well, maybe has a crush on me and is afraid of being rejected."

"If it's online, can you trace it?" Mom asked the detective.

"Depends," Detective Payne answered. "I'll take the information, but some people are better at hiding their real identities than others. And frankly, I have my doubts. Why would someone who's been comfortable communicating on the Internet suddenly decide to leave a handwritten note?"

Mom gestured at the napkin. "What about fingerprints?"

"Not from paper like this," Detective Payne said.

"I don't understand how this person would expect me to show that I can be trusted," I said.

Again, Detective Payne gestured with his hands as if he didn't know, either.

"What should Madison do?" Mom asked.

Detective Payne turned to me. "There's nothing you can do, Madison. Go about your business as usual. Just, you know, be careful. Stay alert." He took one last sip of coffee and reached for the note. "Okay if I take this?"

I nodded. He stood up, folding the napkin and sliding it into his pocket. "It would probably be a good idea if you didn't mention this to anyone, okay?"

"Is there anything new about Lucy?" I asked

The detective hesitated. "We're following several leads."

Mom accompanied him to the front door. She probably had some questions she wanted to ask him. I glanced out the window, where the sun had broken through the gray clouds and light glinted off the Sound. Only a week ago I'd sat in this kitchen not even questioning whether or not I felt safe. After all, this was Soundview. Not only Soundview, but the gated community of

Premium Point. But so much had happened since then—Lucy's disappearance, that awful feeling that someone had been following me in the dark boatyard, and now, this note.

Who could have left it?

The face that unexpectedly appeared in my thoughts was Tyler's.

He knew where I lived.

Rich bitch.

Things like this happen for a reason.

Another voice was in my mind. Dr. Cunningham's: *Did you happen to see anyone else around when you dropped her off?*

I'd said no but now I realized that wasn't true. There *had* been someone else around. Tyler.

Hushed voices drifted down the hall. Mom and Detective Payne were speaking. Then the front door closed and Mom returned. She sat down at the table and took a sip of coffee.

"What did he say?" I asked.

"He thinks someone may be playing with your head," Mom said. "In times of stress, certain, er . . . not well people . . . sometimes do things like this."

"What about Lucy?"

Mom traced the rim of the mug with her finger. "They're stumped. They've brought in dogs and searched everywhere. They've sent alerts to all the neighboring towns. No one's seen her. Her phone hasn't been used since last Saturday. It's as if she just vanished into thin air."

"But he just said they've been following leads."

"I think sometimes the police have to say that," Mom said.

"Just to reassure the public. But Detective Payne just told me that in his thirty years in the police department, he's never seen a case like this."

Even though the house was well heated, I shivered and hugged myself. "It's scary."

"Yes," Mom agreed. "It is."

During the normal IMing and texting that night, I didn't tell anyone about the note. Courtney was online, and I was tempted to try and smooth things over with her, but for once I resisted. Why did I always have to be the one who tried to make things better? Why couldn't she reach out to me?

chapter 10

Thursday 1:14 P.M.

"WHAT DID YOU just say?" Mr. Osmond asked Tyler in current events the next day, the fifth that we would live through without knowing what had happened to Lucy. I'd driven to school that morning wondering how Courtney would get there. Now she sat across the room from me, and neither of us looked in the other's direction.

Mr. Osmond was a new, young teacher with all that enthusiastic "I've got to do more than just follow curriculum" energy that usually lasted no more than the first three or four years.

"I said that some people deserve to die."

The class had gone silent. Everyone knew that this was just the sort of statement that Mr. Osmond loved to pounce on—a seed that he would now water with probing curiosity in the hope that it would blossom into debate. "Deserve to die," he repeated. "So, Tyler, am I to understand that you are in favor of the death penalty, even in cases where the guilty person has not committed murder? In your opinion, these people still *deserve* to die?"

"Absolutely," Tyler replied.

"According to whom?"

"According to what they've done," said Tyler.

Mr. Osmond looked around. "Does anyone agree? Disagree? We're not talking about murder here. The question is, does anyone really deserve to die for committing a lesser crime?"

"Rapists, child abusers, and pedophiles," said Reilly Bloom.

"Damn right they deserve to die," said Jake, and exchanged a high five with Greg Stuart. While he liked to sit with his jock friends in the back of the room, Adam, as a rule, maintained a somber demeanor in class and refrained from the typical dumb-jock hijinks.

"How would you feel if someone decided *you* deserved to die?" Mr. Osmond asked. "Who's to say what constitutes a behavior or crime deserving of the death penalty?"

The class went quiet. Mr. Osmond scanned the room for someone willing to answer. There were certain people he could count on to give an opinion. I was one of them, but today I averted my eyes, hoping he wouldn't call on me.

"Madison?" said Mr. Osmond, as if he could feel my reluctance.

I sighed and gave the answer I'd prepared in my head in case I was called. "I'm not sure I believe anyone has the right to decide who deserves to live or die."

"You'd have let Hitler live?" asked Tyler.

I looked over at him, but unlike previous times when I felt my attraction for him stir, this time I felt wary and uncertain.

"I guess I believe that really bad people should be in prison for the rest of their lives," I said.

"Are you *serious*?" Tyler asked as if I'd just said I believed pigs could fly. "Hitler? You're talking about someone who was responsible for the deaths of six million Jews. Women, children, babies, complete innocents. How can you think someone like that could be allowed to live?"

"Hitler is an extreme case," said Mr. Osmond. "We were talking about someone who has not committed murder."

"If someone intentionally does something that he knows can result in death," Tyler said flatly, "then that person deserves to die."

"Even if he doesn't actually kill anyone?" asked Mr. Osmond.

"It's like everything they've been telling us about bullying since kindergarten," Tyler went on. "You can tease and taunt someone until they're so miserable they kill themselves. Why should people who do that go unpunished?"

It was interesting to me how certain people revealed things about themselves. You could tell that there was something personal about Tyler's statement. I was willing to bet that something had happened in his life to provoke it. Once again I found myself feeling disconcertingly attracted to him. Was it his intensity? His looks? Or maybe it was that he seemed to think and care about something other than what kind of car he owned and where he was going to college?

At the same time I felt the urge to disagree with what he'd said. I raised my hand, intending to say that if you decide to put someone to death, you're no better than they are, but Mr. Osmond looked past me. "Adam?"

Heads turned, perhaps because this was the first time since Lucy disappeared that anyone had heard Adam contribute in class. I glanced out of the corner of my eye at Courtney, but she stared forward, almost as if she'd expected me to look at her.

"People who kill themselves choose to do it," Adam said, looking straight at Tyler. "Nobody makes them."

"That's easy for you to say," Tyler shot back. "I bet you've never been teased or bullied. In fact, if anything, you hang around with the exact sort of mental morons who do most of the bullying in this school. So what would you know?"

The class went silent. It wasn't only the venom in Tyler's words that caught everyone by surprise. It was the way he spoke to Adam. Not just because I couldn't recall anyone ever speaking to Adam like that, but because, as far as I knew, Tyler didn't know Adam at all.

"Let's try not to let this get personal," Mr. Osmond cautioned. "We're having a philosophical debate, okay?"

"Just a minute." Adam stared at Tyler. "I don't know you, and you sure as hell don't know me, but it strikes me that you'd be precisely the kind of person who'd be against stereotyping people. So I would strongly suggest that you reconsider your statement."

Rarely had I heard such calm words delivered with more threateningly ominous portent. It was so unlike Adam.

"Or what?" Tyler asked, staring straight back at him. "I mean, talk about bullying. What are you threatening to do if I don't reconsider? You gonna wait for me out in the hall?"

"He won't, but maybe I will," Jake Barron growled.

"Okay, that's enough," Mr. Osmond said, trying to sound lighthearted and amused. "I'm delighted you both feel so passionately, but if we can't keep this discussion on a cerebral level, I'll have to shut it down, and I really don't want to, so"—he twisted his head around—"how about someone we haven't heard from on this issue? Maura?"

"Oh, come on!" Adam suddenly blurted out.

Once again, the class went silent. A startled scowl crossed Mr. Osmond's face. Everyone knew why Adam had reacted the way he had. Maura was certain to side with Tyler on the bullying issue. Still, it was an incredibly uncharacteristic and embarrassing thing for Adam to do. In the back of the class, Maura stared down at her lap, but she couldn't hide a face that turned bright red. Adam crossed his arms and slid down in his seat, staring at his desk top.

"Maura, what would you say?" Mr. Osmond asked.

Eyes cast downward, Maura stammered. "I—I'd say you could tease someone until they killed themselves. And so it would be your fault. It's happened on the Internet."

Across the room, Tyler nodded as if she's proved him right.

"But," Maura went on, "stereotyping is just as bad."

The class turned to see how Adam would react, but his eyes remained glued to his desk, his face stony.

The bell rang and kids began to get up. "Good discussion today." Mr. Osmond straightened some papers on his desk. "Tyler, would you wait a moment after class?"

As I crossed the classroom, Tyler and I locked eyes. He nodded slightly, as if saying "good fight." I watched as Courtney joined Jen Waits leaving the room, and wondered when, or even if, we'd speak to each other again. Adam left with his friends, his eyes downcast. Out in the hall, I stopped and glanced back into the classroom, where Mr. Osmond was talking to Tyler.

I was still there when Tyler came out. He didn't look

surprised to see me. We fell into step together down the hall.

"So I'm curious," I said. "What did Mr. Osmond want?"

"He likes my willingness to contribute in class but asked that I try to be less confrontational," Tyler explained.

We walked for a few moments without speaking. Usually I would feel the need to fill the awkward silence with some sort of chat, but today I restrained myself.

"So, how're you doing?" Tyler finally asked.

"In regard to what?"

"I don't know. Everything that's going on, I guess. You said you and Lucy used to be best friends."

"Like everyone else, I'm totally freaked," I said.

Tyler hung his head. "You know, I uh . . . I meant to tell you I'm sorry about what happened at the Safe Rides meeting the other day. I should have accepted some of the blame."

I was surprised, and glad, to hear him apologize. "I appreciate that. I'm just curious why you didn't?"

"I don't know. I guess . . . 'cause I'm new here, you know? I'm not sure I want everyone's first impression of me to be, 'Oh, he's a screwup.' And I got the feeling people wouldn't think that of you."

"Well, thanks for saying that. I have to admit it did bother me."

We reached the end of the hall and stopped. "I'm going this way." He tilted his head to the left.

I pointed a finger in the other direction, wishing we didn't have to part. We smiled at each other and I felt those goose bumps again.

"So, uh, you doing Safe Rides this weekend?" he said.

"Yes, I'm on the dispatching desk Saturday night."

"Oh, yeah?" Tyler's eyebrows rose in surprise. "Me, too. We'll be on the desk together."

I felt my smile grow into a grin. "Great. See you then."

We parted and went off in opposite directions. What Tyler couldn't see was that the grin was still on my face all the way down the hall, and into my next class.

There was a message from PBleeker waiting for me at home that afternoon:

I was surprised you didn't point out that Hitler didn't act alone. He needed a lot of help to kill six million Jews. I wonder if Adolf Hitler ever actually killed anyone himself. The weird thing is, you can almost imagine the Nazis were like the most popular high-school clique, lording it over everyone. Then you've got the regular high-school kids, who would be the equivalent of the rest the German population. And then you'd have the outsiders, people like Maura, oppressed and ridiculed like the Jews were, to the point where even the regular kids are afraid to associate with them. Anyone who does is scorned as a sympathizer, just like some Germans were labeled Jewish sympathizers. If you look at it that way, Madison, you're a Nazi. And I have to believe that's not the way you want to be.

Not true, I told myself. *It's just one person's distorted view. Someone who doesn't know what it's like. Someone who only imagines they know.* But it was also creepy, because now I knew that PBleeker was in Mr. Osmond's class.

Str-S-d #9

I wish Adam Pinter would die, because he embarrassed me in class today. It would set a good example. It would be justice. And Courtney Rajwar, too. Because she can't be bothered to be nice to me, while you can see how incredibly important it is for her to be part of the in-crowd, and how hard she works at it. It's just gross the way she sucks up to the popular kids and totally ignores people like me. Like we don't even exist.

....

10 Comments

Ru22cool? said...
Done anything to improve your looks yet, complainer?

Str-S-d said...
Go to hell, Ru22.

IaMnEmEsIs said...
Dreams do come true.

Realgurl4013 said...
You go, giiirl! You're a jeeerk, Ru22.

Ru22cool? said...
Oh, wow, Realgurl, that really hurt! Ow, ouch, ouch! I'm in suuuch pain! Loooser.

ApRilzDay said...
What is WRONG with all of you? You're like a bunch of five-year-olds. And listen, Str-S-d, seriously? You know about KARMA, right? Obviously, writing and wishing someone would die isn't as bad as doing it, but it still sends NEGATIVE ENERGY into the world. And it's also not good for YOU personally. People are attracted to POSITIVE people, and you're not exactly being positive when you're

wishing someone would die. The same goes for the rest of you. Got that, Ru22cool?

Ru22cool? said...
Drop dead.

Realgurl4013 said...
I know negative people can be a drag. But sometimes you can't help it. If people are really mean, you know?

ApRilzDay said...
I don't see how being mean back will make anything better.

Str-S-d said...
It makes me feel better.

chapter 11

Saturday 7:04 P.M.

I SPENT HOURS on Saturday afternoon trying to pick an outfit for Safe Rides that night, wanting to look good for Tyler without being obvious about it. The same went for makeup. Just a little bit of eye shadow, mascara, a touch of blush and lip gloss. I wasn't used to spending so much time on my appearance, and the longer I stared at my reflection in the mirror, the more nervous I felt.

By dinnertime I'd lost my appetite, even though the hearty scent of stew had spread through the downstairs rooms. In the kitchen, Mom and Dad were sitting at the table speaking in hushed voices. As soon as they saw me, they stopped. Mom gave me a nervous "I hope you didn't hear what we were talking about" look. Then her expression changed, becoming more open and curious when she saw that I was wearing new jeans and an oatmeal-colored cashmere turtleneck. "Don't you have Safe Rides tonight?"

I knew instantly what she was implying. "Is it that obvious?" I asked, dismayed by the possibility that I'd overdone the clothes and makeup.

"Maybe only to me," she said, "because I know what you usually wear. So?"

"There's this guy. . . ."

Mom and Dad exchanged surprised, and not displeased, looks.

"Do we know him?" Dad asked.

I shook my head. "He's new this year. And nothing's going on, so can we please, *please* skip the parental interrogation?"

Mom gestured for me to have a seat and served me a bowl of stew from a big pot on the stove. She specialized in dinners that didn't require a lot of oversight, so that she could multitask while the food cooked. Even though I wasn't hungry, I tried a spoonful.

"This is delicious, Mom," I said, then nodded at the big pot on the stove. "But why's there so much?"

"Comfort food for the Cunninghams," she said. "We'll bring it over later. I only wish there was something more we could do for them."

"How are they?" I asked.

"I spoke to Paul today," Dad said. "The police haven't come up with anything solid, and neither has the private detective he's hired. He sounded very low."

"What about the guys at the party from FCC?" I asked.

Dad shook his head slowly. "He didn't mention anything about that."

The conversation turned to preparing the *Time Off* for winter dry dock. Dad planned to spend a good part of the next day at the marina. I listened with one ear and tried not to watch the kitchen clock. I just wanted to get to the Safe Rides office and see Tyler.

The office would open at eight P.M., but I made myself wait until 8:10 before I walked in. Dave Ignatzia was sitting at the desk. I stopped and looked around.

"Looking for Tyler?" he asked. "He called me this morning. Said something last-minute came up and he was going away for the long weekend and could I take his place?"

It was the second night of a three-day weekend. School would be closed on Monday for a conference. The flip side of safe was boring, and you couldn't blame anyone for wanting to get away from Soundview for a few days. And yet I felt like I'd been blindsided. I'd been so focused on sharing dispatching duties with Tyler that night that it had never occurred to me that he might back out.

"Sorry," Dave muttered, and I had no doubt he could read the disappointment in my face.

"Oh, Dave, you have nothing to be sorry about." I forced a self-conscious laugh. "It just, you know, caught me by surprise."

"I guess life's full of surprises," he said with what I suspected was half-veiled resentment.

Inside the Safe Rides office were two old desks with phones to take the calls from kids who needed rides. Spread around the rest of the room were half a dozen mismatched chairs, as well as a small TV, DVD player, and microwave oven. I took off my jacket and scarf and hung them on a hook by the door. Dave cleaned his glasses on the tail of his shirt. For an instant, he looked a little bit like Michael J. Fox, the star of that old movie *Back to the Future*. Then he slid his glasses back on and his eyes became the extra large size I was used to. "You look nice tonight," he said.

"Why, thank you," I said, caught off guard by the compliment.

"Too bad for Tyler, huh?"

I felt an inward grimace. Was it *that* obvious that I'd dressed up for Tyler? Would everyone who came into the office tonight immediately guess the same thing? I sat down. "Let's hope that's the last surprise for tonight."

"He's kind of mysterious, isn't he?" Dave asked.

"Tyler?" I said a bit uncomfortably. "I guess."

"Here's the thing I don't get," Dave said. "How come people want to know more about him, and not about me?"

"I guess because he's new here," I said. "People don't know him."

"And you think you know me? Maybe there's a lot you don't know about me."

"Isn't that true of just about everyone?"

"Some people get more of a chance to show who they are. Other people never get the chance."

We hit an awkward silence. I kept thinking about Tyler. There had to be a million reasons why he'd switched at the last minute with Dave, and surely "hot date" was one of them. But speculating about things I had no way of confirming was a bad idea, and I forced my thoughts back into the Safe Rides office and Dave. "Well, what's one thing you'd like everyone to know about you?"

I don't think Dave expected that question. "Uh . . . I guess I'd just want people to know that I'm a nice guy."

"I think people know that," I said.

"But . . ." Dave began to say something, then must have had second thoughts. Instead he reached into his backpack and pulled out a DVD. "Hey, want to watch *Juno* tonight?"

"Sure," I said, even though this would probably be the dozenth time I'd see that movie about a quirky girl my age who has a baby and decides to give it away. Still, it might help get my mind off Tyler.

The door opened and Ms. Skelling came in, followed by Maura. Our faculty advisor was wearing a full-length shearling with the kind of stitching that had been fashionable in the 1970s or 1980s, and I wondered if it was something she'd kept from her heydays along the Philadelphia Main Line.

"Are we all set for tonight?" she asked while Maura removed her ski jacket.

"I'm taking Tyler's place on the desk," Dave announced. "The driving teams are Maura and Courtney and the lesbians from Mars."

Ms. Skelling frowned. "Keep it to yourself, Dave. Anyone know what's on tap?" She gazed at me as she asked.

"There's supposed to be a kegger in the woods beside the baseball field across from Tony's nursery," I said.

The door swung open again and Sharon and Laurie came in. Sharon was wearing her permanent scowl, which only seemed to increase when she saw Dave on the desk.

"Hi, girls, we're just discussing the plan for tonight," Ms. Skelling told them. "So far we know there'll be a kegger in the woods across from the nursery."

"Jocks," Sharon instantly concluded as she pulled her hoodie over her head. "Well, looks like we'll be busy."

Laurie slumped into a chair without taking off her brown peacoat. Her silent ambiguity always struck me as eerie and unsettling. You had to wonder what was behind that blank look.

"Is there anything else going on that we should know about?" Ms. Skelling asked. She had not taken off her coat and I had the feeling she was eager to get everything settled for the evening so that she could leave. Did she have a date waiting somewhere?

"I heard there's a party at some sophomore's house in the heights," said Laurie.

"Oh, dear," Ms. Skelling said with a touch of resignation in her voice. "We all know what that means. Make sure you have buckets in your cars." She turned to Dave. "The log?"

"Right." Dave pulled open the desk drawer and took out the ring binder where we recorded every call, and the details of each "run" the driving teams did throughout the evening.

Ms. Skelling checked her watch, then looked at me. "We're sure Courtney's coming?"

"She always has to be fashionably late," Sharon sniped.

"She'll be here," I said, even though Courtney and I still weren't speaking.

"All right," Ms. Skelling said. "Have a safe evening. And let's make absolutely sure every client is safely inside their destination before we leave them."

She left, but the echo of her final words remained as a not-too-subtle reminder of my recent failure to follow the rules. The Safe Rides office grew uncomfortably quiet for a moment.

"I don't get it." Dave finally broke the silence. "A party *and* a kegger after what happened last weekend? I would have thought people wouldn't be in the partying mood."

"Aw, look at Mr. Sensitive," Sharon said snidely.

"I think you've got it backward," Dave shot back. "*You'd* have to be totally insensitive *not* to feel that way."

"You think those unenlightened testosterone-addled Neanderthals care about anything except themselves?" Sharon said. "Boy, are *you* in the dark."

Dave glanced at me and I tried to give him a look that said, *Don't take it seriously. It's just Sharon being Sharon.*

"I saw that," Sharon snapped. "God, you're all so smug. So righteous. You make me sick."

Suddenly I hoped there'd be lots of parties that night. Anything to get Sharon out of the Safe Rides office and into her car.

This had been the worst week of Adam Pinter's life. He'd finally gotten up the guts to end his relationship with Lucy. He knew she wouldn't take it well, but who could have anticipated this? Lucy gone? Inexplicably vanished? Adam couldn't shake the feeling that he was somehow responsible. The fight they'd had the night she'd disappeared had been the worst ever. He knew about her condition and the medications she took. But could he really imagine that Lucy would do herself in over him? No, it was inconceivable—condition or no condition. He had never met anyone as grimly determined to succeed. Whatever the prize was, Lucy always had her eyes on it and nothing else. No one knew that better than he. After all, that was what he was to her, just another prize.

But that didn't make him feel any less guilty. If only he'd followed his instincts from the start. Even though Lucy was beautiful and had a killer body, she'd always come across as too serious and determined. Being that he himself was pretty serious and determined, he'd almost always been attracted to girls who just liked to have a good time and not sweat all the serious stuff. So when Lucy had first turned her serious determination on him, he'd known instinctively that the two of them would be a bad match.

And yet, in the beginning there'd been another side to Lucy, playful and sexy and alluring. She was a girl who knew how to get what she wanted, and he'd gradually given in to her subtle but steadfast attention. There was something seductive about feeling wanted, and Lucy had made sure he felt that way.

Until it started to change. It almost seemed that the more confident Lucy was that she had him, the less she thought she needed to try. For the past six months, Adam had felt trapped. The playful, sexy Lucy had morphed into someone he'd privately nicknamed "Mother Lucy," someone who seemed to have their whole life together planned out, only it wasn't necessarily the life he wanted. He understood that part of the problem stemmed from her condition. She couldn't deal with uncertainty. Because dilemmas and ambiguity could easily tip her into depression, she always needed to feel certain and definite. And once he'd been made aware of her condition, he'd felt obligated to do everything he could to help her feel stable and secure.

But gradually, her condition began to overshadow everything they did. More and more he felt like it was his job to make sure she was happy and secure. And strangely, the more obligated he felt, the less happy he was. He was a teenager, for God's sake, and yet sometimes he felt like he was facing a lifetime of taking care of an incredibly hardworking and demanding invalid.

Besides, someone else had entered the picture. Someone interesting and exotic. Someone fun and undemanding who always seemed thankful when he could sneak away to be with her. She was like an oasis, far from the stresses and pressures of his life — the polar opposite of Lucy.

So last weekend at the party, he thought hinting that he was set on going to Harvard might be a good first step. A way of gradually breaking the news to Lucy that it was time for their paths to diverge. But Lucy was too smart. She'd seen right through him. Or maybe it was her realization that there was someone else. Either way, there was nothing gradual about her reaction.

Adam felt a visceral pain born of guilt. All week he'd felt horrible. Had hardly been able to eat or sleep. What if he really had tipped her over the edge? Caused her to do something impulsive and rash, or even worse, calculated and vindictive? It was exactly the sort of thing bipolar sufferers were apt to do, and how else could you explain what had happened? Vanishing without a trace. "No sign of foul play," the cops repeated over and over again. Although Adam suspected that the words were just cop talk for "We don't know squat."

Even the private detective the Cunninghams had hired was coming up blank. He'd met with Adam twice to go over the events of last Saturday night and had prodded him over and over to try and recall anything Lucy might have said to indicate that she was thinking about running away . . . or worse.

Adam had wracked his brain and told the investigator everything. Well, almost everything. He'd seen no reason to bring up the other person. Nor did he reveal that, now that he looked back on it, he wasn't entirely surprised. When Lucy decided to do something, she always had to do it better than anyone else. And if that meant the worst thing imaginable, she'd still go for an A-plus.

"Want to go to the kegger?" Greg Stuart asked.

Riding shotgun in Greg's car, Adam crept back from his

tortured thoughts. They were just cruising around town, enlarging their carbon footprint.

Adam didn't feel like a kegger. He didn't want to be stared at and whispered about, or surrounded by a bunch of self-appointed Florence Nightingales showing lots of cleavage and earnestly telling him how sorry they were for his loss, and how certain they were that everything would work out, especially if he took their phone numbers.

But the one thing a kegger did offer was the opportunity to get royally, obscenely blitzed. He'd lived with this nightmare for a solid week, and he needed a break. Obliteration sounded wonderful.

"So?" Greg said, once again yanking Adam from his thoughts.

"Let's do it."

The kegger was in the woods beside a town ball field that was located behind a small strip mall that included a deli, auto body shop, and hair salon. Adam asked Greg to park in a dark corner of the parking area farthest from the ball field and said he'd stay by the car while Greg scoped out the scene and, hopefully, returned with something to drink.

Adam waited in the car while Greg went off into the dark. Out of the corner of his eye, he saw movement—someone walking across the ball field toward the woods. The silhouette didn't look familiar, but then, it wasn't like Adam knew the gait and profile of every guy at school.

A few moments later, another figure in the dark caught Adam's attention. Greg returned with a forty of Miller Draft and half a bottle of JD. Unfortunately, the bottle of JD was attached to the hand of JB, otherwise known as Jake Barron.

Adam reached for the bottle and pressed the rim to his lips, the first gulp of bourbon burning as it tumbled down his throat, making his eyes water.

"What's up?" Jake asked with a scowl when Adam finally returned the bottle. "How come you're not in the woods with everyone else?"

"Don't feel like it." Adam unscrewed the top from the forty.

Jake shot a puzzled look at Greg.

"Lucy," Greg said.

Jake nodded gravely. "Anything new?"

Adam shook his head and took a big gulp. The cold brew soothed the fire in his throat left by the Jack Daniels.

"Man, that is messed up," said Jake.

Adam reached for the bottle of JD again. "Tell me about it."

The conversation turned to college football but was soon interrupted by loud, girlish laughter coming from the direction of the kegger.

"Sounds like someone's having fun," Greg muttered wistfully, and both he and Jake peered toward the woods behind the base-ball backstop.

Adam took another slug of the JD. This one didn't burn near-ly as much. "Don't let me keep you guys."

"You sure?" Greg asked.

Adam gestured to the forty-ounce bottle of beer. "Just leave this with me."

Jake headed toward the woods. Greg hesitated, studying Adam uncertainly.

"Go on," Adam said. "Have fun."

He stayed by the car and nursed the forty. The beer and bourbon took away the pain, but not the thoughts. Lucy was still there in his mind. He could see her; he just couldn't feel her.

He wasn't sure how much time had passed when Greg came through the dark with his arm around Reilly Bloom's waist. Reilly, a tall girl with chestnut hair and freckles, was the captain of the volleyball team. Adam tipped the forty to his lips and was surprised to discover that it was empty. He didn't remember finishing it.

"Uh, Reilly and I are gonna walk over to her house," Greg said, almost apologetically. "Think you can catch a ride with someone else?"

Adam got the message loud and clear.

At the Safe Rides office, I picked up the desk phone. It was the first call of the night. "Hey, Mads, it's Adam." He was slurring his words. "It's Adam" came out as "Sadddam." "I'm at the deli by the ball field? The one by . . . by the . . ."

"Across the street from Tony's Nursery." I entered the information into the log. "Going to fifteen Sheffield?"

"Where else?"

"Five minutes," I said, and hung up.

"Who was it?" Dave looked over from the other desk. He had the DVD control in his hand and had paused the movie when the phone rang. The two driving teams sitting around the TV raised their heads attentively.

"Adam," I said.

"Maura and I'll go," Courtney blurted out eagerly. She started to rise, then stopped self-consciously when her eyes met mine. She'd finally arrived nearly half an hour late. Neither of us had said hello, but she'd given my outfit and makeup a curious look before settling down on the other side of the office.

Sharon was also getting up. "We already agreed that Laurie and I would do the first run tonight."

Courtney's eyes stayed on mine. I shrugged to let her know that I didn't care who went. But Sharon was already on her feet. "Come on, Laurie. Lesbos to the rescue."

The parking lot in front of the deli was empty. Adam sat on the curb before the dark storefront. His bladder was on the verge of bursting, but he was too dizzy to stand up and go. Each time he closed his eyes, the world began to spin, and he felt like he was going to be sick. So he concentrated on keeping his eyes fixed on the dimly lit Tony's Nursery sign across the street.

But when his eyes focused, his mind seemed to focus as well, and the thoughts he'd drank so much to drown swam back to the surface. Where was Lucy? How did someone just disappear? What could have happened to her?

Just as they had all week, the questions feasted on his flesh, making him feel guilty and resentful. So where was the stupid Safe Rides car? It seemed like he'd been waiting a long time. It should have been here by now.

Above him a thin, gauzy haze drifted in front of the moon, causing a ring to glow dully in the night sky around it. Adam tilted his chin up and studied it. *Thin air*, he thought. What did that mean? If someone could disappear into thin air, did that mean someone could materialize out of it, too?

Courtney's face materialized in his thoughts. That was where he wanted to be right now. In her arms. Wait! She drove for Safe Rides. Hope sprang into his mind and shook itself out like a wet dog. What if she came now? Wouldn't that be a happy ending to a crappy night.

Suddenly, from out of nowhere, a rag with a strong chemical smell was pressed against his face. In the same instant, his head was wrenched hard to the left as if a chiropractor were cracking his neck. Adam felt himself tumbling over onto his side. Whoever was behind him holding the rag to his face was trying to push him down to the ground. His left elbow hit the asphalt parking lot first, sending a searing pain up his arm and through his shoulder. But from deep in his alcohol- and chemically-addled brain, Adam sensed it was also his chance to stop his downward momentum and right himself. Just as he began to plant his hand on the ground to push back up, someone kicked his elbow out from under him. Adam went down, first on his shoulder and then on his back. The next thing he knew, a heavy weight was crushing his chest as if someone was sitting on him. The damp chemical rag was still pressed against his face, and with each struggling breath he took came that horrible, wet, chemical odor.

By the time his bladder involuntarily emptied, Adam was no longer aware of anything. His mind was as black and empty as deep space. Hands slid under his armpits and heaved him up. His heels dragged on the ground as he was lugged around the side of the deli and into the shadows.

* * *

In the Safe Rides office, the evening had started to get busy. Courtney and Maura had gone to get a babysitter who didn't feel comfortable being driven home by the child's father. And a call had just come in from a girl who'd been ditched by her date after a movie and was now waiting at the Cinema 6 for a ride. Dave had paused *Juno* while I wrote the information in the log. When I'd finished, I nodded to let him know I was ready to watch again.

Dave kept the movie on pause. "You like it?" he asked. His glasses slid down on his nose and he pushed them back up with his finger. I wondered why he persisted in wearing glasses that made his eyes look so big. There had to be contact lenses that could have helped.

"Who doesn't?" I said.

"Yeah, it's just about my all-time favorite," he said, once again pushing the glasses back up. "What's your favorite part?"

"Oh, uh, I don't know," I said. "What's yours?"

Dave launched into what I realized was a prepared speech. It had something to do with how *Juno* was more than just a movie, how it was a statement about our generation, and symbolic of our times. I tried to listen, but I knew what I was really hearing was Dave yearning to let me know that he was a deep and thoughtful thinker.

Then my cell phone rang. I made a face to show Dave how disappointed I was that his dissertation had to be interrupted, then answered. "Hello?"

"He's not here." It was Sharon.

"Are you sure?" I asked.

"We're in the deli parking lot and there's no sign of him."

It wouldn't be the first time someone called for a Safe Ride, then changed their mind, but that wasn't Adam's MO. He was too responsible. Even when drunk.

"Could you look around?" I said.

"Already did."

"Hold on, I'll try his cell." With my free hand I dialed his number on the desk phone and held the receiver to my ear. It rang until the message came on.

"Hey, it's Madison," I said. "Where are you?" I put down the desk phone and thought about the girl whose date had ditched her at the movies. "Sharon," I said into my cell. "Go to Cinema Six. There'll be a girl waiting outside. She's going to Evergreen Terrace."

"Roger that." Sharon hung up.

I glanced back at Dave.

"I guess my favorite part is toward the end when Juno comes to the track and tells Paulie she's in love with him," he said. I realized he'd been waiting to answer the question that by now I'd forgotten I'd asked. "And he assumes she means as friends and she says, 'No, for real. I think you are the coolest person I've ever met. And you don't even have to try.' And he says, 'I try really hard, actually.' You know? It's like a moment of truth. Most cool people really do try, don't they?"

Did Tyler try? I wondered. Why, out of the hundreds of possible reasons, was I so convinced that he'd cancelled tonight because of a hot date? Why couldn't I just accept that I didn't know why he'd asked Dave to replace him? Why did I have to make myself miserable by assuming the worst?

"Madison?" Dave said.

"Huh?" I blinked and realized I'd drifted off in thought.

Dave stared at me for a moment, then rolled his eyes and shook his head. "Forget it." He pressed the remote and the movie started to play again.

The urge to apologize instantly leapt to my lips, but for once I restrained myself. Sometimes you can apologize too much, and at that point I was so distracted I wasn't sure what I was supposed to apologize for. What could have happened to Adam? Where was Tyler? What had Dave been saying? Something about his favorite part of *Juno*. The part where Paulie admits that actually he tries really hard.

On the screen Juno was in Paulie's room and Paulie was talking about them getting back together again. I watched and listened as Juno said, "I like you, Bleek, I do. But things are really complicated right now."

She called him Bleek because his last name was Bleeker. . . . Paulie Bleeker.

PBleeker . . . I felt my whole body stiffen. It was one of those moments when a big gong bangs loudly in your head. Pretending to look down at the log, I glanced at Dave. His eyes were riveted on the screen, and his lips moved each time Paulie Bleeker spoke.

chapter 12

"MADISON." I FELT someone shake my shoulder from far, far away. If sleep had been an ocean, I had miles to go before I reached the surface.

"Madison, wake up." The voice and hand on my shoulder were insistent. Some inner clock told me that it was much too early to be awakened. It was still the middle of the night, wasn't it? Or, since I hadn't actually gotten into bed until the middle of the night, it was much too early in the morning.

I opened my eyes. The bedroom was dark. The only light came through the open doorway. Wearing a robe, Mom leaned over me, holding the phone. "It's Ms. Skelling."

Still too sleepy to make sense of what was going on, I took the phone and pressed it to my ear. "Hello?"

"Madison? It's Carol Skelling."

"Oh, uh, hi." *Why would she be calling?*

"I'm sorry to wake you, but Adam Pinter didn't come home last night."

"But it's still dark," I said with a yawn.

"It's ten of six. It'll be light soon. His mother was up all night waiting for him. She's called the police. Is it true that he called for a safe ride?"

I sat up in the bed. "Yes, but he wasn't there when they went to get him."

"Who went?" Ms. Skelling asked.

"Sharon and Laurie."

"Where?"

"The deli by the ball field. That kegger we talked about last night."

"Did they look for him?"

"They said they did." Even in the dimness of my bedroom, I was aware that my mother was hovering over me with an anxious expression on her face.

"So they never saw him?" Ms. Skelling asked.

"That's what they said. Have you spoken to them?"

"I'm going to call right now. Go back to sleep." Ms. Skelling hung up.

There was no chance of that happening. I handed the phone back and felt gripped by fear. Mom sat down on the side of the bed and stroked my hair, trying to calm me, and reassure herself that I was safe. "The Pinters must be worried sick."

"He could have stayed at Greg's house last night," I said, thinking, *or with Courtney*, who had left with Maura shortly after Sharon and Laurie. Maybe Adam was okay. It was entirely possible that Courtney had called ahead and told him to wait for her. And maybe it was conceivable that he'd neglected to call home. After all, he'd sounded really smashed on the phone.

Suddenly, I knew what I had to do, but I had to do it alone.

I rubbed my eyes. "I'm going to try to go back to sleep, okay?"

Mom squinted at me uncertainly, then nodded as if she understood. "Of course." She leaned over and kissed my forehead, then got up and left.

As soon as the door closed, I called Adam, but got his message again. Then I called Courtney.

"Helllllo?" She sounded groggy and disoriented.

"It's Madison. Is Adam there?"

"Huh? No."

"Courts, it's really important."

"Wha . . . ? What's going on?"

"He didn't come home last night."

"Isn't it still last night?"

"It's just before six. Courts, if he's there—"

"He's *not* here, Madison," she said, annoyance creeping through her sleepiness. "I don't know where he is."

"You didn't see him last night?"

"No."

"Or speak to him?"

"No."

Oh, God, I thought. *Oh, no!*

"You . . . think something happened to him?" Courtney asked.

Stay positive, I told myself. *You don't know what's happened. There are other possibilities.* "He sounded really drunk when he called. He could have wandered off and passed out behind a bush."

The line went quiet for a moment. Then she said, "You don't really believe that, do you?"

"No," I admitted, feeling my heart sink. "I don't."

The phone line went silent. I couldn't help wondering whether our disagreement of a few days earlier was just a spat, or the actual end of a friendship. I'd had many friends and acquaintances, but so few best friends. There'd been Lucy, then Gabby Wald, whose family had moved to London after tenth grade, then Courtney. Was there something wrong with me? Something that prevented me from having boyfriends and close girlfriends?

"I'd better go," Courtney said, and hung up.

I lay in bed for a while, trying to recall everything that had happened the night before, especially speaking to Adam on the phone. Was there anything I'd missed? Something he'd said? I thought of that mysterious note. *You and your friends are in danger.*

And now another friend of mine was gone.

The room gradually began to lighten with the coming dawn. Then I had a thought that was so frightening it propelled me out of bed—if Adam was gone in the same way that Lucy had disappeared, then once again, I was the last person to speak to either one of them.

Mom was downstairs in the kitchen with coffee and the newspaper, only the newspaper was unopened. She was gazing out the window at the gray and glassy Sound. I pulled a stool next to her, sat down, and leaned close. Instinctively, she put her arms around me. "What's this?"

I told her what I'd just realized about being the last person to speak to both Lucy and Adam.

She squeezed my shoulder. "Oh, hon, if that's true it's just a coincidence."

"But whoever left that note *knew*," I said. "They said my friends and I were in danger."

Mom just hugged me and didn't answer.

"I'm scared," I said, and trembled.

"We still don't know what's happened," she tried to reassure me. "Don't forget they were—I mean, they are—boyfriend and girlfriend. Maybe they did have something planned."

"Like what?"

"Maybe they decided to run away. Maybe the pressure was too much for them. Maybe she got pregnant and decided to have the baby. Who knows?"

I knew. None of that was true. I knew because of how distraught Adam had been that day he'd talked to me at lunch. I knew because he was a close friend and wouldn't have lied to me when he said he was breaking up with Lucy. I knew because if that was the case, why had someone left that note? I was willing to bet just about anything that Lucy wasn't pregnant and she and Adam had had no plan.

chapter 13

Sunday 7:05 A.M.

Why Lucy, we thought you'd be happy to be reunited with your boyfriend. What, Lucy? Really darling, you must speak up. Oh, we see, your tongue is swollen and it's painful to speak. We know you're weak because you haven't had anything to eat or drink. But look, Adam's waking up again! Aren't you going to kiss him hello? Oh, dear, he's sick. Isn't that too bad? But we guess that's what happens when you drink too much. Come now, Lucy, you can't get that far away from it. So just get used to it.

* * *

BACK UPSTAIRS I sat at the computer. By now, other parents must have awakened their children to ask if they knew anything about Adam, because the text messages and IMs began to fly. The dominant rumor was that Lucy and Adam had planned from the start to run away together. I didn't believe it, but I kept my thoughts to myself.

The one person I wished I could speak to was Tyler. Even though I was still disappointed that he hadn't been around the previous night, this was the sort of thing I felt I could call him about. Or maybe I was just using it as an excuse to connect. I dialed, got his voice mail, and left a message.

After a while, Courtney popped up on the IM list. So now we both knew the other was online. How long were we going to ignore each other? There were times when you had to rise above your pride and do the right thing. I IMed her.

This time, she IMed me right back.

"I don't believe Lucy and Adam ran away," Courtney said later that afternoon. For the moment, or maybe forever, we'd put aside our disagreements. After several days of cold rain, it had turned warm and sunny. Under a blue November sky, we sat at a metal table outside Starbucks, both of us having felt the need to get out of our houses. I wore a hoodie and jacket. I'd looked for my red cashmere scarf at home but couldn't find it, and I wondered if I'd left it in the Safe Rides office the night before. Courtney wore sunglasses. Every few moments she would poke the cuff of her hoodie under the glasses and into the corner of an eye. So I knew she was upset.

"Neither do I," I said. "But you can see how other people might. All the other explanations are so creepy."

Courtney sniffed and dabbed her eyes under the sunglasses again. "I know," she said in a quavering voice, as if fighting not to break down completely. "I mean, what's going on?"

The question hovered uncomfortably in the air between us. From a corner of my mind came the question I still wanted to ask from a few days before—why had Courtney chosen to fool around with Adam?—but I knew this was the wrong time. Searching for something else to talk about, I said, "Anything interesting happen last night?"

"What, with Maura?" Courtney made a face, as if the words *interesting* and *Maura* could not possibly be connected. "She gives me the creeps."

"It's not her fault," I said.

"I'm not talking about the way she looks or dresses. It's the way she *acts*. When you're in the car with her"—Courtney feigned a shiver—"she's so quiet. And if you ask her a question, you get a one-word answer. I always feel like she's sucking something out of me. She's like . . . I don't know, a leech."

"She's shy," I said.

A crooked little smile appeared on Courtney's lips. "You always have to say something nice, don't you?"

Before I could reply, Jen cruised down the street in her car, leaning over the steering wheel and peering at Starbucks. When she saw Courtney and me, she jammed her brakes so hard that she was almost rear-ended by the car behind her. She quickly parallel-parked and got out. Courtney and I shared a "brace yourself" look.

"O-M-G, girls!" she gasped, coming toward us, trying to act somber given the recent news about Adam, but with a telltale glimmer of excitement in her eyes. She pulled a chair to our table. I had mixed feelings about her arrival. It was both an unwanted intrusion and a welcome relief from the shroud of gloom.

"Like, what in the world is going on?" she asked.

Courtney and I shook our heads.

"But you don't believe they planned it, right?"

We shook our heads again.

"It's so weirdly symbolic," Jen said.

"Come again?" Courtney said.

"I mean, the most popular boy and girl in our school?" Jen said. "The king and queen of the prom? The male and female most likely to succeed? The—"

"And your point is?" I interrupted.

Jen leaned close and lowered her voice. "I'm just saying that if something bad happened to them, maybe it's not a coincidence. Don't tell me you didn't think of that?"

Courtney and I shared a surprised look. Neither of us had.

"We don't know that anything bad's happened to either of them," I said.

"Oh, right." Jen smirked dubiously. "They've *both* just vanished into thin air. Happens every day. And by the way, you realize Lucy's now been gone for more than a week?"

Neither Courtney nor I answered. It was hard to imagine that there was anyone in Soundview who *wasn't* aware of how long Lucy had been missing. Jen rose from her chair. "Be right back." She went into the Starbucks.

Courtney stared past me and up the block where Greg, Reilly, and Jake were coming down the sidewalk. Greg's and Jake's hands were jammed into the pockets of their jeans. All three of them had grim expressions on their faces.

A little while later, there were six of us at two tables pushed together, huddled over our coffees.

"This is unreal," Jake muttered. "I mean, stuff like this doesn't happen around here."

"You know, the night Lucy disappeared," said Greg, "there were some guys I'd never seen before. I heard later that they were from FCC. And there was at least one guy at the kegger last night who I'd never seen before. Maybe—"

"Oh my God!" Reilly gasped, sweeping her chestnut hair out of her face. "I know who you mean! I talked to him!"

We stared at her.

"Last night. At the kegger. I can't believe I didn't put it together until now." Reilly pressed her hand to her chest as if to keep from hyperventilating.

"What did you talk about?" I asked.

"I don't know, just stuff," Reilly said, although from the distant look in her eyes you could see that even as she answered, she was still searching her memory. "I'd had a couple of beers and I talked to a lot of people. I'm trying to remember."

"Was he from FCC?" Greg asked.

"I don't think he said," Reilly answered. "I mean, he definitely wasn't from our school. I sort of assumed he was from some school nearby."

"What kind of stuff did you talk about?" Courtney asked.

"Well, he wanted to know who was who—"

"And that didn't seem weird to you?" Jen interrupted.

"Not at the time. I mean, he didn't know anyone so he was asking, that's all. Just making conversation. It's seemed pretty natural."

"And you're sure he never said where he was from?" I asked.

Reilly stared at her coffee. "If he did, I don't remember. . . ." She looked up as if she'd just remembered something. "He wanted to know who the most popular kids were."

For a moment, all of us exchanged shocked looks. "Oh . . . my . . . God!" Jen muttered.

I flipped open my phone and called the police.

It wasn't long before a dark green sedan pulled up and Detective Payne got out and came toward us.

"Do you know what happened to Adam?" Jen asked.

"I think it's best if I ask the questions," Detective Payne replied patiently. He turned to me. "Madison, you said you have a friend who might have some important information?"

I introduced him to Reilly.

"You spoke to this person?" Detective Payne asked her.

Reilly nodded uncomfortably.

"Remember what he looked like?"

"Sort of. It was kind of dark."

Detective Payne glanced around at the rest of us and then focused again on Reilly. "Would you mind coming down to the station? I'd like to ask you some more questions, and maybe you could give us a description."

Reilly gave me a nervous glance, but I nodded back reassuringly.

She turned to the detective. "Should I, like, tell my parents?"

"Certainly," said Detective Payne.

While Reilly called her mom, I asked Detective Payne if we could speak in private for a moment. We walked a dozen yards down the sidewalk.

"Thanks for calling me," he said in a low voice. "This could be helpful."

"I was thinking about the note," I replied. "It said that my friends and I were in danger. Adam is one of my closest friends."

Detective Payne nodded. I didn't have to spell out the rest for him: It didn't sound like a joke anymore. It didn't sound like someone just wanted to play with my head. It sounded like who-ever wrote that note knew in advance that something was going to happen to Adam.

Reilly came toward us and handed the phone to Detective Payne, who assured Mrs. Bloom that this was perfectly normal and her daughter wasn't in any trouble. I went back to the table and watched as Detective Payne escorted Reilly to his car and held the door for her.

"I don't believe it," Jen said for the twentieth time.

"It's pretty obvious that detective thinks this mystery guy is involved somehow," said Jake.

"Like how?" Jen asked.

"Who knows?" said Jake. "It's a little weird that first the guy would do something to Lucy and then come back for Adam."

"I'd say it's more than just a *little* weird," said Courtney. "It's totally weird. Like in the stuff-like-this-only-happens-in-movies category of weird."

I listened with only half an ear. Whoever had left that note had known that Lucy, Adam, and I were friends. That didn't sound like something some "mystery guy" could have figured out just by talking to kids at a party or a kegger. It seemed a lot more likely that the note had been written by someone who knew us. I was wondering about that when, halfway down the block, a familiar-looking purple car went around the corner. It was Tyler, who'd told Dave he'd be away this weekend.

The rest of us stayed at Starbucks and talked. Cell phones rang as friends called to find out where people were, and gradually the group sitting at the tables on the sidewalk swelled to more than a dozen. It was something I couldn't remember us ever doing before. We often got together at school, sports events, and parties, but never on a Sunday afternoon outside Starbucks. I wondered if people felt there was safety in numbers. I also wondered what was going on with Tyler. The fact that he was still around and hadn't gone away strengthened the "hot date" theory, but with no way of truly knowing, I forced myself to stop thinking about it.

A little while later, Reilly returned and told us how, at the police station, they'd asked her some questions, but that she'd spent most of the time with an artist at a computer trying to come up with a face that matched the "mystery guy" from the kegger.

We sat and talked a little longer. By now it was late afternoon and the sun had gone below a building and cast a shadow over us. The sidewalk began to feel chilly.

"So what about tonight?" Jake asked Courtney. There'd been talk on Friday that since there was no school on Monday, some people might gather at her house Sunday night for what was termed more of a get-together than a party. But that idea had been floated before Adam had disappeared.

"Does anybody really still feel like it?" Courtney asked.

"It beats hanging around at home," said Greg, and others nodded in agreement.

Courtney gave me a curious look.

"I might stop by," I said. "But first I have to muck out Val's stall, and I'm supposed to have dinner with my folks." Then I had another thought. "One other thing, guys? Whoever goes out tonight, try to stay in pairs—like a buddy system, okay?"

It had not been my intention to remind everyone of the frightening circumstances surrounding our lives at that moment, but that's the way it felt. People started to drift away.

"Give me a ride home?" Something about the easy way Courtney asked made me think that she wanted to make up. We got into my car and she said, "So you still want to know why I went with Adam?"

"Only if you want to tell me."

Courtney looked out the window. "Maybe you were right. Maybe it was because Adam was Lucy's boyfriend. So being with him . . . and knowing he wanted to be with me? Even when he was with *her*?"

I was glad that she'd decided to tell me—but sorry, too. One reason I'd become friends with Courtney was because she had that wild and unpredictable streak—the opposite of me, Ms. Predictably Unwild. Her lack of restraint was kind of enviable considering how restrained I'd been brought up to be. But it had never occurred to me that she'd do something so well, of course it was self-serving, but it was also so . . . out-of-bounds. In my mind, cheating with another girl's boyfriend could not be justified, no matter who he or she was.

Courtney tilted her head against the headrest and glanced at me. "Angry?"

"No, not angry. More confused and disappointed, and really worried about him."

"I know . . . but seriously, Madison? I could tell he didn't want to be with her. You know that look guys give you."

I nodded but secretly wasn't sure. Had I ever gotten that look? "Just because a guy gives you a look . . . I mean, you must get that all the time."

"Not from Adam Pinter."

I pulled into her driveway. The house looked dark and empty. Her father was probably away on business, and her sister at her boyfriend's. No wonder Courtney wanted company tonight.

"Try to come by later, okay?" she said. "I don't know what we'll do, but I'm pretty sure it'll be low-key. It just feels like right now is a time when you want to be with your friends."

Soundview Stables was at the end of a dirt road. You parked in a lot at the bottom of a small hill and walked up to the two identical stables, painted red with white trim. When I got there, Mr. Farnsright, the overnight manager, was coming out of the west stable, the one where we kept Val.

"Hey, Madison." He waved when he saw me. "Gonna do a little evening mucking?"

"Is that okay?" I asked apologetically. "I know it's almost dark."

"No prob," Mr. Farnsright said. "Just be sure to lock up when you're done."

"Thanks." I turned toward the stable door.

"Oh, Madison?"

"Yes?"

"What's this I hear about kids disappearing? That true?"

I nodded.

Mr. Farnsright slid his cap back and scratched his head. "Strangest thing I've ever heard. You know, a detective came by here today, asking about halothane." He could tell by the face I made that I didn't know what he was talking about. "It's a chemical vets use to anesthetize animals. Wanted to know if we had any of the stuff, or if I knew who might. I said we didn't, and the only folks I could imagine having it would be the local vets, like Dr. Harris and Dr. Costello."

Inside the east stable a horse neighed, and a bat darted through the dark above us.

"Well, g'night, Madison. Don't forget the doors." Mr. Farnsright headed up the hill toward his house and I let myself into the stable. What could an animal anesthetic have to do with Lucy or Adam disappearing? I wondered. It was maddening to think about. Another possibility to mix in with all the others. Maybe all of it was coincidental. No, surely the note implied that wasn't the case. Wasn't it obvious by now—because she'd been gone so long—that something bad had happened to Lucy? And somehow I knew something bad had happened to Adam, too. Because he wouldn't have wanted his family to worry. That's just the way he was.

Inside the stable I mucked out Val's stall and thought about seeing Tyler in town a few hours earlier. There were probably lots of explanations for that, and yet it made me feel uncomfortable. Why did I have to have a crush on him of all people? Why couldn't I have picked someone a little more predictable and easier to figure out?

I finished mucking, and started to groom Val, running the rubber curry comb down the horse's flanks. There was something soothing about taking care of my horse. Once I got into the rhythm of combing, it took me away the way sailing took my father away. The stable began to feel like a world of its own, far from school, social pressures, inscrutable guys, and from friends disappearing. It was just me and Val and the long, even strokes down her brown flanks.

It was dark by the time I finished. I said good-bye to Val and left the west stable, latching the door behind me. Outside, the air had grown chillier, and I paused to watch my breath come out in a cloud of vapor. Suddenly I heard whinnying and banging from inside the east stable across the yard. It could have been a horse cribbing or weaving in its stall, but it sounded too frantic.

A nervous shiver ran across my shoulders. Something was wrong, but what should I do? I stared at the east stable's red door, my feet frozen to the ground.

"Hello?" I called. "Is someone in there?"

No answer. The whinnying grew louder. A second horse had joined in the fray. Something was seriously spooking them. What if it was a fire? My stomach began to knot. I stepped closer to the east-stable door, hoping to hear something inside that would give me a clue. But all I heard was banging and the clopping hooves of agitated horses.

"Is someone in there?" I called more loudly. "Is something wrong?"

No answer.

I was scared, even though I told myself I shouldn't have been. I'd been coming to these stables since I was a child and knew everyone who worked here, as well as most of the people who boarded their horses. I made my feet step forward and forced my trembling hands to reach for the stable door.

Just then the banging and neighing inside stopped.

I felt a welcome relief. I didn't have to look inside now, did I?

Suddenly the frenzied sounds started again. I jumped and backed away from the stable door, only to realize that this time the cacophony was coming from somewhere else. Somewhere behind me.

The noises were coming from the west stable . . . where Val was.

Without a moment's hesitation, I ran to the stable door and threw it open. The horses inside were wild and bucking. Down at the far end something dark moved. Door hinges squeaked loudly. By the time I focused on it, whoever had been there had gone through. *Bang!* The door slammed shut.

I ran down to Val's stall. Like the other horses, she was weaving and whinnying, but nothing appeared to be the matter. I heard a creak and spun around. *Bang!* The other stable door slammed shut. I fought the impulse to run to it. My heart was banging and I took deep breaths trying to calm myself.

I walked slowly toward the door and pulled the handle. But

it didn't open. It was latched shut from the outside. I was locked in, trapped.

Fright rose in my throat. A cry began to gather in my chest, but I stifled it, then pulled out my cell phone and dialed Mr. Farnsright's number.

The next few minutes were some of the longest I'd ever experienced. The horses calmed down, but I didn't. Stomach in knots, heart thumping, trembling from head to foot, I waited.

Finally the stable door began to open. I took a fearful step back and held my breath.

There stood Mr. Farnsright with his bushy eyebrows in a deep V. "What's going on, Madison? How'd you get locked in here?"

"Someone . . . must have locked me in."

He frowned. "Who'd do that? There's no one else around."

"There was. And I don't know why." I stepped out into the cold air. The night had grown quiet.

Mr. Farnsright closed the door behind me. "You saw someone?"

"I thought so. It happened so fast. You didn't hear the horses?"

He shook his head and looked around again. "Seems pretty quiet."

It was obvious that he doubted my story, and for a moment I was tempted to try to convince him. But how? And even if I did, what was the point? I glanced at the dark dirt road that led down to the parking lot and began to feel nervous again.

"Mr. Farnsright, would you mind just walking me down to my car?"

The night stable manager frowned again, but then nodded. We went down the road. My car was the only one in the lot. At first everything looked fine. Then I noticed something odd. The car seemed lower than normal. The front tires were slashed.

"What's going on?" Dad asked later, while driving me home from the stables. Mr. Farnsright had stayed with me until he'd arrived.

"I don't know, Dad," I said. "I'm really sorry about the car."

"That's the least of my worries," he replied. "The garage will come get it in the morning. What I want to know is why you went to the stables alone."

"I always do that," I said.

Dad slid his eyes toward me and pursed his lips hard. "For God's sake, Maddy, given what's been going on, do you think that was a good idea?"

He was right. "Sorry, Dad. I didn't think."

"Why would anyone slash your tires?" Unlike Mr. Farnsright, Dad didn't doubt for a second that someone else had been there upsetting the horses, and had locked me in. He drove silently through the dark, but I knew his mind was processing, assessing, and considering.

Finally he said, "We need to decide what to do."

"About what?"

"First Lucy, then Adam, and now this. Mom told me about the note. Do we keep you home? Or send you and Mom away someplace safe until whatever's going on passes? I won't take any chances with you, hon. You're too precious."

"But we still don't know what's going on. Maybe my tires were slashed by mistake. Maybe whoever did it thought I was someone else."

But I could see Dad didn't believe that. "I'm worried about kidnappers," he said. "Lucy and Adam both come from well-to-do families. Just because a ransom demand hasn't arrived yet doesn't mean one won't come soon."

"But what about the note?" I asked. "And don't kidnappers usually just kidnap one person at a time? Have you ever heard of something like this happening before?"

"I'm not sure you can apply the word *usual* to what kidnappers do," Dad said. "What I do know is that kidnapping has changed. It's become an international problem with drug cartels and terrorists getting involved. The terrorist angle is especially worrisome because it accomplishes two goals. They can get money for their activities and strike fear into the hearts of people everywhere. You know that's always been one of my greatest concerns."

M. Archer and Company was known for being associated with people of great wealth. While other kids were learning to look both ways when crossing the street, I was being taught what to do if I was ever kidnapped. What the general public didn't know, and the police only suspected, was that the kidnapping of the children of wealthy parents happened more frequently than was reported in the news. Most wealthy families were much more concerned with quickly paying the ransom and getting their children back than solving the crime, and so the police were rarely notified. Instead, special "intermediaries" were used to negotiate ransom demands and deliver the agreed amounts. Only the lawyers of wealthy families seemed to know who these "intermediaries" were.

"I don't want to go away, Dad. You have my word that from now on I won't go anywhere alone."

He didn't reply. As we drove through the dark, I thought of something else. "Have you ever heard of an animal anesthetic called halothane? Something veterinarians use?"

"No. Why?"

"A detective was at the stables this afternoon asking Mr. Farnsright about it. I have to think it has something to do with Lucy and Adam, but I can't imagine what."

Dad was quiet again and I knew he was thinking about it. Finally he shook his head. "Sorry, hon. I don't have a clue."

* * *

Str-S-d #10

Something weird is going on. I wished Lucy would die, and then she disappeared. Then I wished Adam would die and I just heard that he's disappeared. It has to be a coincidence, right?

....

💬 **10 Comments**

Realgurl4013 said...

It can't have anything to dooo with you, but it serves 'em right, if you ask meee.

ApRilzDay said...

That is TOTALLY weird, but I agree, it has to be some kind of coincidence. You can't hold yourself responsible. But just between you and me, I think it could also be a SIGN that it's time for you to STOP wishing people would die.

Tony2theman said...

This is so cool!

Tweenypie said...

My friend Tony told me to read this blog. Is this true? OMG! It's so amazing! I mean, what if you have THE POWER?

Tony2theman said...

Where R U, Str-S-d? Could you come to my school? I've got some people you could get rid of for me.

ApRilzDay said...

I REALLY don't think this is funny. And I don't think Str-S-d thinks it's funny, either. Maybe you guys could LAY OFF, okay?

Tony2theman said...

Who asked you?

Axel said...

This is BS. This Str-S-d chick made the whole thing up. It's just a big attention grab. That's why she'll never say where she is.

ApRilzDay said...

I believe her. There could be A LOT of reasons why she won't tell where she lives.

Axel said...

Yeah, right. Uh-huh. Sure.

You say she won't wake up, Adam? That's too bad. You want us to do something about it? What would you suggest? Oh, Adam, aren't you being silly? Now, don't get angry. See what we have in our hand? You know what happens when we use it. Oh, dear, what a nasty thing to say!

Oooh, it hurts when we do that, doesn't it? So we think you'll have to apologize for what you just said. Not ready? You will be.

Yes, look at you with tears in your eyes. We wonder how many people have ever seen the great Adam Pinter cry. Yes, we thought you'd apologize after that. Why are we doing this? Because you deserve it, that's why.

What did you do to deserve it? We think you know what you did. We all can't be born handsome and strong and talented like you. Didn't you ever, for even a minute, stop to think about how fortunate you are?

Or, should we say, *were*?

chapter 14

Tuesday 8:50 A.M.

WHEN SCHOOL REOPENED on Tuesday morning, Mom had to drive me because the Audi was still in the garage. But we had an unexpected surprise. Mobile TV vans were parked on the street outside the school entrance and reporters were doing news reports with the school in the background. Groups of kids had gathered to watch.

"I don't like this," Mom grumbled as we drove past. "I want you to stay away from those cameras and go straight into the building."

"I know, Mom."

She stared through the windows at the news crews and sighed. "Don't they realize this is only going to make it worse?"

In homeroom, Ms. Skelling was sitting at Mrs. Towner's desk.

"Where's Mrs. Towner?" someone asked.

"She's had to start her maternity leave early," Ms. Skelling answered. "Don't get too comfortable. You'll be going to an assembly in a few moments."

"What's going on?" asked Maura.

"It's about the missing kids, dummy," Jake snapped. "What else?"

"That was completely uncalled for, Jake," Ms. Skelling scolded. "You can apologize to Maura immediately or go directly to Mr. Edwards's office."

The class went silent. Glowering, Jake hunkered down at his desk. Across the room, Maura's face grew red.

"Well?" Ms. Skelling demanded.

"I'm *so* sorry, Maura," Jake snarled sarcastically.

Ms. Skelling narrowed her eyes. "You think I'm joking? Not only will you go to the office, but you'll sit here every day after school for the rest of the semester. Which means you can kiss lacrosse good-bye."

Jake grimaced and stared down at his desk. "I'm sorry, Maura."

"That's better," said Ms. Skelling. "I don't know how Mrs. Towner ran this homeroom. But you will refrain from calling each other names in my presence. Especially during a crisis like this. We will treat each other with dignity and respect."

The announcement came over the PA to go down to the auditorium for the assembly. I ran into Courtney in the hall.

"We missed you last night," she said.

After what happened at the stable, I'd completely forgotten about the get-together. I decided not to tell her about my car. Things were already code red in the gossip-and-rumor department. "How was it?"

Courtney shrugged. "Pretty much what you'd expect. Everybody's freaked. But it was better than being alone, I guess."

We got into the auditorium and took our seats. Wearing a dark blue suit, white shirt, and red tie, Principal Edwards stepped up to the podium on the stage. "I assume you all saw the media when you came to school this morning," he began. "Unfortunately, there's nothing we can do about them as long as they stay off school property. We'll just have to live with them until this situation resolves itself."

He paused while murmurs rippled through the audience, then continued: "As I'm sure you all know by now, another student disappeared over the weekend. I don't want to alarm you, but I would be acting irresponsibly if I didn't take prudent steps to protect students until we all understand what's going on. To that end, I am recommending that all of you participate in a voluntary curfew beginning each evening at dark."

The fact that there wasn't a single groan or peep of protest from the crowd in the auditorium was a sign of how seriously everyone was taking the disappearances of Lucy and Adam.

"If you must go out at night," the principal continued, "I urge you to go with a friend or family member. Under no circumstances should anyone be out alone after dark. In addition, I would strongly suggest that you make every effort to curtail parties and keggers and all other forms of get-togethers that involve the consumption of alcohol."

The principal paused and, in the silence that followed, the kids in the audience looked around as if expecting at least one wise guy to make a crack. But no one said a thing.

"On a more positive note," the principal went on, "we don't expect this situation to go on much longer. I spoke to Police Chief Farley this morning, and he told me they are making progress in the investigation. They have now identified a person of interest who they are eager to speak to. As you leave after the assembly,

you'll be given a sheet of paper with a sketch and some information. If you have seen this person, or know anything about him,
please come to the school office immediately. You may go. Please
proceed to your first-period classes."

As everyone got up, whispers and muttering flittered through
the auditorium. "This is unreal," Courtney mumbled. "It's like,
can this really be happening? Here? I'm waiting for someone to
pinch me."

"At least they're making progress," I said as we inched our
way toward the aisle, packed with kids slowly making their way
toward the exits. Among them was Tyler in his black trench coat.
Our eyes met, and he paused and waited for us. Despite all that
was happening, I felt myself growing excited and nervous at the
prospect of speaking to him.

"Crazy stuff, huh?" he said when Courtney and I joined him
in the aisle.

"Totally," Courtney agreed.

He gazed at me, as if awaiting my reply. "I thought we were
going to be on the dispatching desk together on Saturday night,"
I said.

"Oh, uh, yeah." Tyler averted his eyes and stared at the floor.
"Something came up."

"Dave said you suddenly decided to go away for the weekend?"

"Uh, right," Tyler mumbled, as if he'd forgotten.

I knew he was lying because I'd seen him in his car on Sunday
afternoon. Then again, it wasn't as if we were in a relationship where
he was required to tell me the truth. We were hardly even friends at
this point. But still, it irked me. No one likes being lied to.

At the exit, we were each handed a sketch of a man wearing a baseball cap. He was described as being about 5'10" and weighing approximately 170 pounds. He had brown eyes and wavy brown hair. One of his front teeth had a chip in it.

"I bet this is the description Reilly gave at the police station," Courtney said as we headed down the hall.

Tyler stopped. "She *saw* the guy?" He seemed especially startled.

"At the kegger Saturday night," Courtney said. "Before Adam vanished. He asked her who the popular kids in the grade were."

Tyler's brow furrowed, and I wondered why this news would have such an impact on him. Our eyes met. "This is too strange to be true," he said, although to my ear it sounded forced, as if he thought that was what we would expect him to say.

We kept walking. I felt torn between my attraction for him and my apprehensions. There was so much I didn't know about him. Was it foolish to let myself feel the way I did?

Then, unexpectedly, Tyler said, "Hey, Courtney, think I could have a word with Madison in private?"

Courtney gave me a quick, searching look to make sure I wanted to be alone with him. I nodded, and she said to Tyler, "Be my guest," then gave me a wink and angled off.

"You angry at me or something?" he asked once she was gone.

"What makes you think that?"

"Just the way you're acting."

I decided to be honest. "You told Dave you were going away for the weekend, but you were in town on Sunday afternoon."

Tyler seemed taken aback. "Yeah, well, I felt like I had to give him a good reason to take my place."

"So you lied?"

He frowned. "Whoa, maybe I lied to *him*, but not to you. I mean, what's the big deal? Tell me you've never made up an excuse to get out of something last-minute?"

He was right. People made up excuses like that all the time. So maybe I wasn't really upset because he'd lied. Maybe I was upset because he'd chosen to do something else rather than be with me. By now we'd reached my physics class. "I'm, uh, in here," I said, once again feeling mixed up and uncertain.

"See ya," Tyler replied tersely, and continued on, clearly annoyed.

I knew I wouldn't see him again until lunch, and spent most of the morning trying to think of what I could say to make things better between us. Finally it was lunchtime, and I walked to the cafeteria more quickly than usual, only to be disappointed when he wasn't there.

"Did you hear what happened after the assembly?" Courtney asked when I sat down. "A bunch of kids went to the office. Like, they *all* say they saw or talked to this guy? And it was always the same thing? He wanted to know about the popular kids?"

I stared at her, wide-eyed. So it *was* possible that the "mystery guy" had learned that Lucy, Adam, and I were friends. And that meant he could have left the note at the guardhouse. But why?

"I mean, how completely freaky is that?" Courtney asked.

I was too distracted to answer. The police were looking for

this person because they believed he had something to do with Lucy and Adam. But I'd gotten the note *before* Adam disappeared. Why would the person who left the note want to warn me ahead of time that my friends were in danger? It seemed like that would have been the last thing he'd want to do.

"Hello?" Courtney gave me a little wave. "Earth to Madison?"

"Sorry, I was just thinking about something."

"Duh. So what did Tyler want before?"

It was an effort to drag my thoughts from one mystery to another. "Oh, I don't know," I said, feeling frustrated that he wasn't in the cafeteria.

"Something wrong?"

I told her how I'd accused Tyler of lying when it wasn't even me he'd lied to.

Courtney let out a "when will you learn?" sigh. "You don't get guys to like you by accusing them of lying."

Nodding woefully, I agreed. "I know. It was stupid."

Courtney stared past me and her expression changed. Jen came out of the lunch line with Tabitha Madrigal and Cassandra Quinn and started toward us. "Look who's bringing reinforcements," Courtney muttered under her breath.

"Hi, girls," Jen said cheerfully when she reached the table. "Okay if Tabitha and Cassy join us?"

I smiled and said hello to them, but Courtney was less enthusiastic. Not because she disliked the girls, but I imagined because she was irked by Jen's blatant plan to step into the vacuum left by Lucy. As if Lucy was gone forever.

"So what do you think of the voluntary curfew?" Jen asked

with a slight roll of the eyes to let us know what she thought of it.

I didn't answer. Tyler had just entered the cafeteria. He took a seat by himself at a table near the window and opened a book. I purposefully didn't stare, mostly because I didn't want Jen to notice and start gossiping and spreading rumors about who I might be interested in. But then I felt Courtney's elbow gently nudge my side.

"Be right back." I got up and headed for the lunch line, then circled back toward Tyler's table, hoping Jen wasn't paying attention. Tyler was busy reading a book titled *SERIAL KILLERS: The Method and Madness of Monsters*.

I breathed deeply to calm my nerves and stood across from him until he looked up. He frowned, and then seemed to force an uncomfortable smile as he closed the book.

"No lunch?" I said.

"That's what you came over here to say?" Tyler's face was expressionless.

"No. I came to say I'm sorry. What you tell Dave is none of my business."

Tyler blinked as if he was surprised. "Okay, thank you."

I glanced back at my table where Jen was busy gabbing. She hadn't noticed me standing across from Tyler, but she might soon. "Would you mind if I sat?"

"It's a free country."

I sat down and tapped the cover of the book. "Interesting reading."

When Tyler nodded but didn't reply, I began to feel even more uncomfortable. "Well, I just I wanted to say I was sorry.

Didn't mean to interrupt." I placed a hand on the table and started to get up.

"Don't go," he said. "What do you think is going on?"

"I wish I knew." I nodded at the book. "That's what you're thinking?"

Tyler shrugged. "It's just an interest of mine."

"Serial killers? That's not exactly in the same league as video games or fantasy sports. What's so interesting?"

"I guess because they're just so different. So outside the norm."

"You like things like that, don't you?"

"I wouldn't say I *like* it," Tyler said. "Maybe I'd just like to understand it. It's a lot more interesting than what's inside the norm. Although, you'd probably disagree. You probably like the norm because it's safe."

He was baiting me again. Only this time, it was easy not to rise to the bait. "Not necessarily. Sometimes the norm can be pretty boring. But right now, anything safe sounds really good."

Tyler nodded. "True that."

It felt like the conversation was flowing more easily, and I was tempted to steer it toward the things I was curious about—Where was he from? Why had he moved here a month after school began? But before I could ask, a commotion began on the other side of the cafeteria. Voices rose in alarm. Heads began to turn and people stood to get a better look. A small crowd had bunched up, and a lunch monitor was telling people to move back. The cafeteria doors opened and Principal Edwards hurried in, followed a few moments later by the school nurse. More kids went to see what was going on, and now Principal Edwards's voice joined the lunch monitor's in telling everyone to move away. Some kids started back to their tables.

"What was it?" Tyler asked one of them.

"Looks like Maura fainted," the kid said.

Gradually, except for the grown-ups and some kids around Maura, the cafeteria began to return to normal. Things briefly got exciting again when two paramedics arrived with a stretcher. But then the bell rang and Principal Edwards told everyone to go to class.

chapter 15

Thursday 9:00 A.M.

MAURA WASN'T IN school the next day. By Thursday morning, it seemed almost everybody had forgotten about the incident in the cafeteria and was once again focused on Lucy and Adam. But when I got to homeroom early and found Ms. Skelling marking papers, I decided to ask. "Have you heard anything about Maura?"

Ms. Skelling looked up at me with a slightly astonished expression on her face. "Do you know that you're the only one who's asked?"

The comment made me feel self-conscious. "I was just wondering. That's all."

She hooked her thick red hair behind her ear. "You needn't apologize. There's nothing wrong with caring about someone who's not in your crowd. She's much better, thank you. I expect she'll be back at school tomorrow."

"Okay, thanks." I started to turn away.

"Madison?"

I stopped. "Yes?"

"You're one of the few young people in this school with any manners."

"Well . . . it must be from my parents, you know?" I backed out of the room. "But thanks."

"You're welcome," she said, and looked back down at her papers.

During a free period in the afternoon, I went to the library to research a paper on Shakespeare's tragedies. Dave was sitting on a couch, reading a *National Geographic*. He glanced up briefly, his eyes large behind his glasses.

"PBleeker?" I said.

His face went blank, then slowly formed a scowl. "Sorry?"

"That doesn't mean anything to you?"

"Should it?"

"Paulie Bleeker? From *Juno*?"

Dave's lips parted into a smile. "Right. Sorry, I didn't get it. So . . . ?"

Either he wasn't PBleeker or he was a very good actor.

"I'm glad you brought the movie to Safe Rides the other night," I said. "I'd forgotten how good it was."

"The best," he agreed. "I mean, like, everybody knows it's hard to be a teenager, right? And you think you're the only one who feels that way even though you know that can't be true. And then there's that line where Juno says—"

"'I think you are the coolest person I've ever met. And you don't even have to try,'" I quoted. "And Paulie says, 'I try really hard, actually.'"

Dave grinned. "You remembered!"

"You told me a few nights ago," I reminded him.

"But I didn't think you were listening." He shrugged sheepishly.

"I was. It's a great line. Do you really think it's true?"

"No—I mean, yes. It's just that some of us, the harder we try, the less cool we are. The problem is, if we don't try, we're not cool, either. In fact, no matter *what* we do, we're not cool."

I felt a smile grow on my face. "That's funny."

Dave beamed. "Yeah, you know, I thought it would be funny? And I wanted it to be funny? But I was also being serious. Does that make sense?"

"I guess so."

He grew quiet, and I wondered if he was practicing every sentence in his head before he said it. Then he said, "Okay, Madison, the truth is, being a dweeb really sucks. And now you're going to say, 'But Dave, you're not a dweeb.'"

I laughed again. "And then what do you say?"

"I insist I'm a dweeb and then we get into a big argument over whether I'm a dweeb or not."

"Who wins?"

"I don't know. Maybe it ends with a standoff. Or a dweeboff. Only I don't know what a dweeboff is and I only said it because I thought it might sound funny, and if it sounded funny, maybe you'd think I was cool, only we've already established that I can't be cool." He took off his glasses and cleaned them with the tail of his shirt.

"Did anyone ever tell you that you look a little bit like Michael J. Fox—the actor from *Back to the Future*, remember?"

The unexpected burst of laughter from Dave's lips was loud enough that people around the library looked up from what they were doing. Dave ducked down behind the *National Geographic*.

"Wow, Madison," he whispered, "your credibility just went straight down the toilet."

"I don't think so. I bet if I've noticed, other people have, too."

"Oh, yeah," he said. "At least a dozen people a day. And that's not counting all the people who tell me I look like Zac Efron and Kevin Jonas. I'm telling you, Madison, with all the attention I get, sometimes it's hard just being me."

"Are you always this funny?" I asked.

"Well, actually, no."

We both chuckled, then grew quiet. I waited to see if he had anything more to say, but he didn't. "Well, guess I better get to work." I got up, then turned to look at him.

Dave was squinting up at me. Only now he didn't look quite as much like Michael J. Fox. "Thanks, Madison," he said.

After school, Laurie drove them home. As they turned the corner, Sharon saw the dark green sedan parked in her driveway. "Pull over!"

Laurie pulled her car to the curb and gave Sharon a quizzical look. Panic swept over Sharon. She felt as if her temperature had just risen five degrees. She bit her lip until it hurt. "Tell me that isn't an unmarked police car."

Lest there be any doubt, the Costellos' front door opened and a thin man with a blond moustache walked down the path to the car and got in.

"Oh, God," Sharon groaned. Her insides turned upside down. She was certain she'd been busted. That little creep

Maura had narced on her. She was totally screwed.

The dark green sedan backed out of the driveway and started in their direction.

"Duck!" Sharon gasped, and hunched down beneath the dashboard. She looked up at Laurie, who hadn't budged. "Come on!" Laurie didn't move. "What are you doing? He'll see us!"

"He's gone," Laurie said calmly.

Sharon poked her head up over the dashboard just enough to see. The street was empty. She slid back up to the passenger seat. "What's wrong with you?"

Laurie gave her a droll look. "Would you chill, please?"

"You don't think that was a detective?" Sharon asked. "You don't think they asked Maura in the hospital where she got the ketamine? You don't think my parents are going to kill me the second I walk into my house?"

"You don't know," Laurie replied.

Sharon flipped open her cell phone and called Maura's house. She wouldn't be able to say anything over the phone because Maura had warned her that her mother listened in on her conversations, and Maura had to be the only teenager in the world without a cell phone. A woman answered.

Sharon made an effort to sound friendly. "Hi, is Maura there? This is her friend Sharon from school."

A moment later Maura got on. "Hello?"

"Hi, I have that book Mr. Osmond asked us to read," Sharon said. "I'm not far from your house and this would be a good time for me to drop it off."

The line went quiet and Sharon held her breath. If Maura

had anything more than the brains of a toadstool she'd understand that Sharon wanted to see her.

"Okay," Maura whispered.

Sharon made Laurie drive her to Maura's place. Maura came out wearing a stained white sweatshirt with a tear in the collar. *What a loser,* Sharon thought as she opened the car window. In a low voice she said, "You told the police where you got the Special K?"

Maura looked surprised. "No, I didn't."

"They didn't ask you at the hospital?"

"They did, but I said I'd had it for a long time and couldn't remember where I got it."

That was a smart answer, but it sounded too smart for Maura.

"You're lying," Sharon said.

"No, I'm not."

"Then why was there a detective at my house just now?"

Maura frowned. "How would I know?"

Sharon stared at her uncertainly. "If I find out you're lying, I will kick the crap out of you." She turned to Laurie. "Let's go."

Laurie started to drive. "Think she was telling the truth?" Sharon asked.

"Yes."

"Then why was that detective at my house?"

"Why don't you go find out?"

On the way home, Sharon's insides began twisting again. She was surprised at how terrified she was of getting in trouble with the police and amazed to discover that she was equally afraid of what her parents would do. Suddenly her big plan of going to San

Francisco felt like nothing more than a crazy fantasy. How could she have believed that she'd go all that way alone? Where would she live? What would she do? How would she support herself?

They pulled into her driveway. Sharon began to tremble from fright. She turned to Laurie. "Would you come in with me?"

Laurie nodded.

"Promise me you won't leave unless everything's okay?" Sharon asked.

Laurie put her hand on Sharon's. "I promise."

Friday 8:43 A.M.

THEY PUT NEW tires on the Audi. In the morning when I got in, I noticed something on the passenger-side floor and felt my breath catch. It was another folded plain white napkin. With shaky hands I unfolded it:

PEOPLE ARE STILL IN DANGER. WE NEED TO MEET AND TALK. YOU HAVE TO LET ME KNOW THAT I CAN TRUST YOU.

The Audi had been locked and the windows closed. It would have been impossible to slide the note in. Since no one had touched the car since it had come back from the garage, that meant someone had put the note in it between the time the tires were slashed and the car was returned to our house.

I glanced at the dashboard clock. If I wanted to get a coffee before I picked up Courtney, I'd have to get going. It wasn't long before I was parked in Courtney's driveway, sipping my café macchiato and waiting for her to come out. But my thoughts were mostly on the note. How could I let the writer know I was trustworthy if I didn't know who he or she was? But something else bothered me. Everyone wants to think that they're trustworthy, so naturally, if someone asks you to prove it, you want to. But what if this was a trap? Maybe I *didn't* want to be trustworthy for this person. I found myself wondering what Tyler would say. Tyler saw things differently. I wished he was there in the car with me. I wanted to know what he'd think.

I glanced at the clock and realized five minutes had passed. Where was Courtney? Her house looked dark and quiet, but it always looked that way. I called her on my cell phone but only got her message.

Had she overslept? Of all the wild and irresponsible things Courtney was apt to do, this wasn't one of them. Not that she was compulsive about being on time; she just didn't seem to need much sleep.

So now what? I called again. And again got her message. It was possible that she'd let the battery in her phone run down. I tried the home phone and got another message. The next step would be to knock on the door, but at the thought of it, I felt my stomach get tight and my heart begin to thump.

What if something's wrong?

Don't be silly. Nothing bad can happen if you just go to the front door and knock.

But I couldn't help picturing the front door opening and someone else being there, waiting to grab me. I reached into my book bag, took out the Safe Rides folder, and dialed Tyler's number.

"Yeah?" he answered after the first ring.

"Hi, it's Madison. Sorry to bother you. Are you already at school or still on the way?

"Actually, I'm kind of running slow this morning. Why?"

I told him where I was and asked if he'd stop by on his way to school. Another ten minutes passed before his car pulled into the driveway behind me. I got out of the Audi. "Thanks for coming."

"No prob." He looked up the driveway at the vast ranch house and the large lawn that surrounded it. "What makes you think she's there?"

"I pick her up every morning," I said. "If she wasn't there, she would have called and told me."

Tyler took a deep breath and let it out slowly. "Okay, let's go see."

We walked up the driveway, past Courtney's VW Bug under the light green tarp, to the front door. Tyler rang the doorbell and waited. There was no answer. He rang it again.

"What about her parents?" he asked.

"Her mom's in India taking care of a sick grandmother and her father's a traveling salesman. He's usually only home on weekends."

"There's no one else?"

"A sister in law school. She's supposed to come home at night, but she usually stays with her boyfriend."

Tyler knocked loudly on the door. If anyone was inside, they would have heard. A queasy, uncomfortable sensation began to spread through my stomach.

"Know where her bedroom is?" Tyler asked.

"Yes, but—"

He jerked his head. "Come on."

We walked around to the back of the house. Tyler gazed out at the tennis court and pool in the large backyard. Since it was a ranch, all the rooms were on the ground floor, but the bedroom windows were above eye level.

"I think it's this one." I stopped under a window with green curtains.

Tyler reached up and knocked on the glass. The queasy feeling continued to grow in my stomach. When Courtney didn't come to the window, Tyler reached up to the ledge and pulled himself up, trying to peek through a crack in the curtains.

"I don't think she's there," he said, lowering himself.

Oh, God, now what? I thought, my insides convulsing.

As we walked back around the house to the driveway, I began to feel like I might throw up—something I hadn't done in years. "I just hope she's at school," I said, but at the same time I knew the chances were slim. How would she have gotten there?

Tyler didn't answer. I wished he'd say something reassuring, but he didn't. We got in our cars and he followed me to school, my stomach cramping the whole way. "She has homeroom in the physics lab," I told him when we met again in the student lot. I started toward the entrance, not realizing how fast I was walking until I noticed that Tyler was practically jogging beside me.

We got to the physics lab and I pushed open the door without knocking. Sitting at his desk, Mr. Stanton, the physics teacher, frowned.

"Is Courtney here?" I asked.

"I've marked her absent," Mr. Stanton said. "Shouldn't you be in your—?"

I turned away and started quickly down the hall. Tyler fell into step beside me. I felt like I was on autopilot, moving fast and trying not to think but thinking just the same. *This can't be happening. It just can't be. Not again. Not to Courtney!*

In no time Principal Edwards had one secretary trying to track down Courtney's father and sister and another secretary on the phone to the police. Tyler and I sat in the main office. My heart was trying to force itself into my throat and I felt so sick I wasn't sure I could move. *This can't be happening,* I kept thinking. *It just can't!*

Principal Edwards paced between the two secretaries, then looked at me. "Who else could possibly know where she might be?"

"Maybe Jen Waits," I said.

The principal turned to a secretary. "Get Jen Waits down here, pronto." He turned back to Tyler and me. "You two go to class."

I heard what he said, but it didn't process. *Go to class? At a time like this? Why? What for?*

Tyler touched my arm. "Come on, we better go."

I went with him out into the hall. Everything was spinning and I felt light-headed. With each thump of my heart, the word *no* thundered in my head. *No! No! No! Not Courtney!*

"There have to be explanations we're not thinking of," I heard myself say in the hallway. "She could turn up in an hour and everything will be fine."

I wanted Tyler to agree, but he said nothing. It was almost as if he knew something I didn't know. Was that possible? Or was I slowly going insane imagining crazy things?

Down the hall, a classroom door opened and Jen came out. "Oh, uh, hey, guys." Her smile and greeting were both subdued.

"Do you have any idea where Courtney is?" I asked.

Jen turned pale. "No. Why?"

I explained that she wasn't home or at school. "That's why Principal Edwards wants to see you. Did you talk to her last night?"

Jen's eyes darted left and right, and I could tell she knew something. She nodded slowly. The little color left drained out of her face. "Oh my God," she half-gasped, half-whispered.

"What?" I asked.

"Some of us got together at Greg's house last night. We just, you know, felt like hanging out. We didn't stay late. Like not past ten. When it was time to go, Courtney said she'd walk. A couple of us said we'd drive her, but she said it was dumb because she lived on the next block."

Tyler and I stared at each other. That was not the explanation we were hoping for.

* * *

Oh, isn't this fun? Now that there are three of you, we can have a party. Sorry, Adam, you say Lucy is cold? Yes, we always thought she was. Yes, Adam, we know that's not the way you meant it. Oh, please, Adam, don't be so hard on Courtney. She has a right to cry if she wants. Frankly, we thought you'd be delighted to have your two favorite women beside you.

Did you just call us a sadistic psychopath? Oh, my, such harsh words! Oh, now, don't try to grovel or apologize. We know that's what you always do. Don't you know that once the words are out, the damage is done? You can't apologize away the hurt you cause. You can't go around thinking that just because you apologize, everything goes back to the way it was.

* * *

Dad always had Frank at Soundview Gulf work on our cars. A small, wiry, bald man, dressed in neatly pressed olive green coveralls, Frank had a reputation for being honest and hardworking. Part of the reason he worked so hard was because it was difficult in a place like Soundview to find young people willing to be pump jockeys or assistant mechanics. Parents didn't want their children taking part-time jobs at the garage when they could be doing schoolwork, or playing sports, or pursuing music or theater or whatever.

I found Frank under a car on the lift, removing a long rusty pipe.

"Hello, Madison," he greeted me. "Everything okay with the Audi? Not having a problem with those new tires, are you?"

"No, they seem fine, thanks."

Frank gave me an uncertain glance, clearly wondering what I was doing there. "So, how can I help you, young lady?"

"Were you the one who got the car from the stables?" I asked.

"Yep, that would be me." Frank reached up under the car again.

"Do you happen to remember seeing a folded white napkin on the passenger-side floor?"

"Nope. Are you missing it? 'Cause we don't take anything out of cars, even the ones that come in with more garbage in them than a sanitation truck."

"No. I found it in the car this morning and wondered how it got there."

"Well, we don't eat in cars, either," Frank said with a smile. "So it's a hard one to figure."

One explanation was that the person who'd slashed the tires had left the note. Once I'd seen that the tires were slashed, I'd never looked inside the car. But why would anyone slash my tires and then leave a note saying that people were still in danger and we needed to meet and talk?

There was another possibility, as well. "After you put the new tires on the car, you put the car in the lot next to the garage, right?" I said.

"Yep."

"Was it locked?" I asked.

Frank stopped working and looked at me again. "Might have been, but I couldn't say, Madison. I mean, it was just a napkin, right? No harm done?"

"No, Frank, no harm done. I was just wondering how it got there. That's all."

Frank gave me a puzzled look, as if he couldn't understand why anyone would care so much about a napkin. "Sorry I can't help you, Madison."

"It's no problem." I turned to leave. "Sorry to bother you."

"Say hello to your folks for me," Frank called from behind.

I got in the Audi and left. At the intersection, I stopped at the light and looked in the rearview mirror. A purple car had just pulled into the gas station and Tyler got out, wearing olive green coveralls.

Str-S-d #11

This is the last blog I'm writing. I'm really scared. I wished three people would die, and now they're all gone. I don't believe anymore that it's a coincidence. Someone's been reading this blog. Someone crazy enough to do what I wished for. If you're reading this right now, you know who you are. You're the one person in the world who is always nice to me. But today in school you said something. I'm not sure you even realized what you were saying, but it totally creeped me out. Now I don't know what to do. I could go to the police, but they'll want to know how I know and then they'll find out about this blog and blame me. The parents will blame me. Everyone will blame me. Everyone already hates me. But this is the worst thing that ever happened. Maybe I should kill myself. I could kill myself, but then someone would figure it out. I don't want to be blamed for this. Even if I'm dead.

....

💬 2 Comments

Realgurl4013 said...
> OMG! This is the thing that's been on TV! I saw it! You go to that school? Unreeeal!

ApRilzDay said...
> I saw it, too. You HAVE to go to the police and tell them. What if those kids are still alive? What if that person has them? Even if it's too late, do you want that person to GET AWAY with what they've done?

chapter 17

WE'D ALL HEARD of schools being locked down, but this was the first time I'd ever heard of an entire town being locked down. At least, that was the way it felt. As soon as word about Courtney's disappearance got out, everything went on total red alert. Some parents insisted on keeping their kids at home. And most of those who didn't insisted on driving their children to and from school and then keeping them home for the rest of the day.

Not that anyone really minded. We were all scared. Three kids had disappeared. Even if we'd been allowed to hang out, nobody wanted to go into town, which was swarming with reporters and TV crews. There were a few kids who got off on being interviewed and seeing themselves on TV. But at school most people reacted coldly to the idea of using such an awful situation for any kind of personal gain or glory. Besides, after you told the media that you were really scared and definitely not going out at night or anywhere alone, what else was there to say?

There was a new message from PBleeker:

Think it's a coincidence that the kids who've disappeared
were three of the most popular in the grade? Check this
out: http://www.journalnews.com/vtm/news/article/murder_
unsolved

I was taken to the Web site of the *Shawnee Mission Journal News*,
a newspaper that served a suburb of Kansas City:

ONE YEAR LATER MURDER MYSTERY STILL UNSOLVED

Every morning when Ellen Woodworth wakes up, the first thing
she wishes for is to go back to sleep. When that doesn't work,
she imagines her daughter, Megan, coming into the bedroom and
saying, "Hey, Mom, what's up?" And then, every morning, Ellen
Woodworth cries.

One year ago, Megan, a popular and vivacious senior at Shawnee
Mission High School, disappeared from a party, never to be seen
or heard from again. Her disappearance came roughly two weeks
after her best friend, Molly Lincoln, mysteriously vanished after
being dropped at her house by her boyfriend late at night.

A few months later, a hunter discovered Molly's remains in some
woods about five miles from her home. Aside from an undisclosed
"mutilation" the police refuse to divulge for fear of compromising
their investigation, her remains showed no other sign of trauma
or poisoning and medical examiners were unable to identify the
exact cause of death, although traces of an animal anesthetic
called halothane were found on her clothes.

Despite repeated and extensive searches, Megan Woodworth's
body has not been found.

Sitting in her kitchen in this well-to-do suburb of Kansas City, Ellen Woodworth talks about what life has been like for the past year. "We live between misery and despair and hope. There's no in-between. Sometimes I feel like I'm breathing, but I'm not alive. I'm taking care of things, but nothing makes sense. One of the things I hate most is how Megan's brother and sister are suffering because I can't be the mother to them that I once was."

There are other frustrations as well. Despite the fact that Molly and Megan were best friends and disappeared within weeks of each other, the police have not been able to connect the two incidents. "Obviously, it's very tempting to say the two cases are related," says Shawnee Mission Police Chief Edward James. "But right now we have one unexplained death that appears to be murder, and one missing person. If we knew for certain that Megan had been abducted, or was the victim of foul play, we might be able to conduct the investigation differently. But we have no leads and nothing to go on. People ask, 'Are you still looking for her?' and our answer is, 'Where do we look?'"

Ellen Woodworth shares Chief James's frustration. "We both want to get Megan back and we both want to stop whomever was behind this from doing it again," she said. "Chief James has given me access to all kinds of databases. I look at them all the time because they're constantly being updated. I wish he could give Megan's case more of his time, but he has a police department to run, and, of course, Molly's parents need answers, too."

Unlike Ellen Woodworth, Molly Lincoln's parents do not vacillate between hope and despair. For them there is only despair. "We still can't understand it," said Howard Lincoln, a prominent Shawnee Mission lawyer. "Molly was a popular, fun-loving girl. Everybody liked her. Why would anyone do this to her?"

The story sounded disturbingly familiar. Halothane was involved. Both girls were popular. Mysterious mutilation? What could that be about?

The problem with texts, e-mails, and phone conversations is you can't see the face of the person you're talking to. Most of the time it doesn't matter, or you can use emoticons, but I wanted to talk to Tyler, and I wanted to see his face when I did.

Dad was away on a trip and Mom had an important board meeting at the hospital. Since I wasn't allowed to go anywhere at night, I called Tyler and asked if he would come over.

"Why?" he asked, sounding surprised.

"I have to talk to you about something."

"Well, here I am. Talk away."

"In person, Tyler. Please? It's important."

Half an hour later, the guard called me from the gatehouse and asked if it was all right to let Tyler Starling through. I said it was and waited by the front door while he drove up the driveway and parked in the circle. He got out of his car and gave me a perplexed look. "Hi."

I held the door open for him. "Thanks for coming."

Tyler stepped into the house and looked around with that slightly wondrous expression most people displayed on their first visit. Sometimes people said, "Quite a place you have here," or "Nice digs," but Tyler preferred to remain silent. I led him into the kitchen, and he gazed out the windows at the glass-enclosed indoor-outdoor pool.

"Someone likes to swim?" he asked.

"My mom, mostly. Would you like something?"

"Sure. How about, 'Why did you want to see me?'"

I gestured for him to sit down at the kitchen table. "You work at the garage?"

Tyler leaned back and stared at me. "That's what you called me here to ask?"

"I'm just wondering why you didn't tell me."

"Oh, sure, Madison, that's just what I'd want everyone to know. That I'm a closet gearhead. Then I'd really fit in around here."

"I thought you didn't care about fitting in."

"Look, I'm not ashamed that I work there, okay?" he said. "I just don't see the point in broadcasting it. You know people have preconceived notions about the kind of guys who like to work on cars."

I couldn't help a small smile.

"What's so funny?" he asked.

"You're just"—I wasn't sure how to say it—"complicated."

Tyler smirked.

"Did you change the tires on my car?" I asked.

He frowned. I could see that he had no idea what I was getting at. "Matter of fact, I did. Why? Did I do something wrong?"

"Did you also leave a note in it?"

He scowled. "No."

"You *sure*?"

"I think I'd know if I left a note. Why? What did it say?"

I didn't want to tell him. Instead, I said, "Tyler, where do you come from?"

Consternation deepened the furrows in his forehead. "What is this?"

"I'm just asking where you come from."

"Why? And why am I being interrogated by you? Am I under suspicion for something? Who gives you the right to ask me this stuff?"

"Is there a reason why you won't tell me where you come from?"

He placed his hands on the table and started to get up. The part of me that was attracted to him didn't want him to go. But the part of me that was frightened of him did. I watched him stand, and good manners dictated that I do the same. I followed him out of the kitchen and down the hall toward the front door. All kinds of things whirled around in my head. I felt tempted to apologize for being nosey, but I did want to know where he was from, and I didn't feel that was something I had to be sorry about.

He reached for the door, but it was locked and he wound up yanking haplessly at the handle.

"Let me do it." I opened the door and turned to face him. The cold air rushed in around us. This was as close as we'd ever stood. Our eyes locked and suddenly everything changed. He gave me a curious, uncertain look. It was like neither of us was sure what we were doing. But I was no longer wondering where he was from, or what had happened to my friends. I was only thinking about how many times in the past month I'd imagined this moment.

His face moved closer, then stopped, as if he was asking if it was okay.

I closed my eyes and lifted my mouth to his. A moment later I felt his lips on mine.

It was a long, passionate kiss. The kind of kiss you don't want to end. Since it was completely unexpected, I was surprised, but even more surprised by the urgent passion I felt from Tyler. He slid his arms around me and pulled me to him. Was it possible that he'd been yearning for this as much as I had? I put my arms around him, felt his back under my hands as I pressed against him. I wasn't thinking about anything except this moment—this kiss, this embrace—and staying in it as long as I could.

It was only the cold that made it end. Tyler pulled his lips away. "You're shivering."

"It's okay," I said, my arms still around him, not wanting to let go.

Our eyes met again. This time, his were softer but no less intense. "Listen to me," he said in a low voice. "There are things . . . you don't know about. You have no idea what's going on. The best thing you can do is stay out of it. Don't go to parties. Not that there'll be any from now on. Don't go anywhere at night, especially alone."

He started to back away, but I held on to his jacket. "If you know something, why don't you go to the police?"

He shook his head. "No way. I have to go."

Tuesday 1:07 P.M.

"HAS ANYONE READ this story?" Mr. Osmond held up the local paper featuring a headline about the police bringing in an FBI profiler to help them with the case. A few hands went up. One of them was Tyler's. This was the first time I'd seen him since we'd kissed. In the midst of all these terrible developments, I felt privately embarrassed that I'd spent so much time thinking about his lips on mine. But I was frightened and uncertain, too. He'd hinted that he knew something about what was going on. How was that possible? And why, I wondered, hadn't he even looked in my direction since the class began?

"What did you think of it?" Mr. Osmond asked.

"Do we *have* to talk about this?" asked Reilly. "I mean, can't we just for one class not think about it?"

Mr. Osmond sent a searching gaze around the rest of the class as if asking if we agreed.

"Doesn't matter what else you talk about, we're still gonna be thinking about what's going on," said Greg. "I mean, how can anyone *not* think about it?" He pointed out the window at the line of media vans parked across the street. Others around the room nodded in agreement. A shroud of anxiety, fear, and sadness had settled over the school. Teachers tried to get on with the normal task of teaching, students tried to learn, but mostly we were just going through the motions.

Mr. Osmond turned to Reilly. "If it would make you more comfortable, I can give you a pass to the library."

Reilly sighed as if to signal her displeasure. But she didn't take the pass.

Mr. Osmond pointed at the newspaper. "According to the FBI profiler, the suspect is almost certainly a male, probably in his twenties, white, and a loner."

"Why does he have to be a male?" Sharon asked.

Mr. Osmond turned to the class. "Any answers to Sharon's question?"

"Maybe because he had to be strong enough to subdue some-one like Adam?" Jake guessed. "He was a pretty big strong guy."

Greg raised his hand. "Don't you mean, Adam *is* a pretty big strong guy?"

This crisis had made people change in unexpected ways. Greg, who had always come across as a cutup who cared about sports and partying and little else, had become morose and thoughtful ever since his best friend disappeared.

"I think there are plenty of women who could handle Adam if they wanted to," Sharon stated and glanced at Laurie, who nodded.

What a strange pair, I thought. *Not because they're a couple, but because one is so belligerent and the other so docile.*

"Maybe it's not one person," Dave pointed out. "Maybe it's two."

Everybody assumed he was referring to Sharon and Laurie.

Sharon made a face at Dave, who smiled back smugly as if he thought he'd won that round.

"So let's talk about profiling," said Mr. Osmond. "Clearly this FBI profiler is basing his assumptions on data gathered from past situations similar to this one, and on the suspects who were eventually apprehended."

"But we *still* don't know what happened to Lucy, Adam, and Courtney," I said. "When you talk about past situations, you're talking about serial killers, aren't you? We don't know if they've been killed."

Again, I glanced at Tyler. He was staring straight ahead. Wouldn't it be natural for him to look at me since I was the one speaking? Especially since I'd brought up serial killers?

"I agree with Madison," Greg said. "If I was in their shoes, I think I'd be really ticked off by some of your assumptions."

"Wait a minute," said Dave. "Isn't it possible that the cops know a lot more than we do? If they've brought in this profiler, isn't it because they have reason to think that Lucy, Adam, and Courtney have been the victims of foul play? I mean, why else would they do it?"

"I'm sorry, but I think this is really sick," said Reilly. "We have no idea what's going on. We're talking about our friends like they're topics in some lesson plan, not real people."

Mr. Osmond pursed his lips thoughtfully. "I understand what you're saying, Reilly. I thought we might as well talk about this, since it's what we're all thinking about anyway. Personally, I believe the subject of profiling has implications that reach far beyond what's going on here in Soundview. But this is a difficult situation for all of us. We don't have to talk about it."

The class was silent. I had a feeling that everyone knew that what Mr. Osmond said was true. No matter what we talked about, the only thing we would really think about was what happened to Lucy, Adam, and Courtney.

"We might as well talk," said Greg. "At least it'll make the time go faster."

Reilly raised her hand. "Can I still have that pass to the library?"

Mr. Osmond went to his desk and wrote her a pass. "Does anyone else want one?" he asked.

No other hands went up, and Mr. Osmond returned to the front of the class. "So what do we make of this? Can human beings really be narrowed down to a predictable profile?"

The class was stony quiet. Mr. Osmond began to look around. I hastily tried to formulate an answer. I felt like I could have argued either way—for or against profiling. But then I thought about Tyler. He would almost certainly be against it.

"Madison?" Mr. Osmond called on me.

"I think it's wrong," I said. "It's just like stereotyping."

"But we all stereotype, don't we?" Mr. Osmond asked. "How many of you have been in an airport and saw someone who looked Middle Eastern and felt nervous that this person might be a terrorist? Or walked down a block at night and saw a black man approaching? Or saw some guy come to school wearing a long black trench coat?"

Murmurs riffled through the classroom and eyes shifted toward Tyler, who raised his hand. "It's my favorite coat."

"What do you imagine people think when they see you wearing it?" Mr. Osmond asked.

Tyler shrugged. "I don't care. Only, you know what? I actually do think you can profile people. I've done some reading about school shooters. And they're almost always male and loners."

"What about a trench coat–wearing male loner who isn't a school shooter?" our teacher asked. "And all the Middle Easterners who aren't terrorists? Is it fair to profile them?"

I raised my hand. "Maybe that's the problem. Profiling is only reactive. You can look at someone *after* they've done something bad and see how they fit the profile. But there are so many others that fit the profile that you can't really use it to predict."

Tyler's and my eyes met. It was difficult to read his expression. I wished he'd smile at me. I wanted to know that kiss had meant something to him. Something lasting.

"But profilers would argue that you can use profiling to narrow down the number of suspects," Mr. Osmond said.

"To white male loners?" I almost laughed. "You could round up dozens from this school alone."

"Maybe it's worth it," said Greg. "I mean, if it could save another . . . person from disappearing."

"You can say that because you're not a loner, Greg," I countered. "But suppose you were? How'd you like to be rounded up just because you fit a profile?"

"Hey, if it meant saving a life," said Greg.

"And suppose it meant you missing lacrosse season?" I asked.

Greg blinked, as if suddenly the real implications of profiling had hit home. Tyler nodded approvingly. That felt good, and I smiled back. It wasn't much, but it was something.

"Very good, Madison." Mr. Osmond turned to the rest of the

class. "I know it isn't easy to focus right now, but I appreciate you for trying. Thank you, those who participated and those who listened."

Class ended and an ache hit me. I hadn't thought about Courtney all period. I was so accustomed to her being there to walk out with. But she wasn't there. It was unbelievable. Once again my eyes met Tyler's. He gave me the slightest smile. We left the classroom together.

"That was interesting," he said.

"I don't know about you," I said, "but I crave those few moments each day when I actually forget what's going on. Even before Courtney disappeared, it was like a nightmare you couldn't wake up from. Now it's even worse."

Tyler didn't reply. Maybe he thought I was just making conversation. Maybe he was lost in his own thoughts about the things he'd implied I didn't know about. I took his sleeve, stepped to the side of the hall, and lowered my voice. "I need to ask you something."

Tyler stopped. I stood up on my toes and he bent down. "It totally bothers me that you implied that you know what's going on. If that's true, you seriously have to go to the police. People's lives are at stake, Tyler. It's not some kind of game."

He stared at the hallway floor. "They already know what I know."

That caught me by surprise. "How do you know?"

I could see that he was struggling, as if part of him wanted to tell me. "Listen, Madison, seriously, if I could tell you, I would. I know it's not easy, but you have to believe me when I tell you it's best if you stay out of it."

"But I don't understand," I said. "What are you saying? That you're going to handle this by yourself?"

Tyler's face suddenly hardened. He abruptly started to walk away. I wanted to reach out, but something told me not to.

With lunch coming up, I stopped at my locker to drop off some books. When I closed the locker door, Maura was standing there. "Ah!" I gave a little gasp and felt my heart jump. Maura frowned, and I wondered if she thought there was something about seeing her that made me gasp. "Oh, gosh, you surprised me." I placed my hand on my chest. "I didn't know you were there. Everyone's so jumpy these days."

Clutching some binders against her chest the way little girls sometimes hugged teddy bears, she nodded. I wished that for just once she would look me in the eye.

"Hey," I said, recalling what had happened a few days before. "How are you? What happened the other day? Is this your first day back?"

Still staring down, she said, "I, uh, wasn't feeling well."

Since when does the school call an ambulance for a student who isn't feeling well? I wondered. *Usually we go to the nurse.*

"So what's up?" I asked uncertainly, since this might have been the first time she'd ever approached me.

"I don't want to bother you," Maura started hesitantly, "but there's something . . . I want to tell you. I picked you because you're different than the others. You've never been mean or anything."

"Uh, thank you," I said, although I wasn't sure I understood what she was talking about.

"It's about what's been going on," Maura said, still staring downward. "But if I tell you, you have to swear you won't tell anyone. Not a soul. Can I trust you?"

Trust me? I felt a jolt of realization. Was she the one who'd been leaving those notes?

"Maura, I'm not sure I can give you my word," I said, "if it has anything to do with what's going on. People's lives could be at stake. I mean, not just could be. Are."

"I know," Maura said. "But you have to swear. It's the only way I can tell you."

I thought about Courtney, Adam, and Lucy, and decided that I had to hear what she had to say. And if I had to, I would break my promise. What choice did I have? "Okay, Maura, I . . . I swear I won't tell a soul."

Maura stepped close and spoke so quietly I could barely hear her. "I wished they would die. I wrote about it."

"You . . . *wished* Courtney, Adam, and Lucy would die?"

Maura nodded. "They were so mean."

A question popped into my head: "Are they dead?"

For once Maura gave me an open, wondrous look. "How would I know?" But then she seemed to realize what she'd done and again averted her eyes.

Can you blame me for feeling confused? "So that's all you did? You just wished they would die? But you don't really have any idea what's happened to them?"

She shook her head. Students passed us in the hall, some giving us curious looks. *Poor Maura,* I thought. Didn't she know that she surely wasn't alone? There had to be lots of kids who'd wished someone popular would die. "I'm glad you told me. I wouldn't worry about it."

Maura scowled and her lips parted as if she were going to say something more, but she changed her mind. I had the strangest sensation that there was more to the story. "Is there . . . something else? Something you're not telling me?"

For an instant her eyes widened with surprise, and that's when I knew she wasn't telling me everything. I was almost certain of it. But before I could ask, she mumbled something about getting to her next class, and hurried away.

Almost every day, a few kids snuck away during lunch to go to the 7-Eleven and buy the late edition of the local newspaper. That's how I learned why the police were asking about halothane. They'd found traces of it on a rag in the parking lot in front of the deli—the last place Adam had been seen. The police theorized that someone might have used the anesthetic to subdue Adam.

"Listen to this." Jen had the newspaper spread before her on the cafeteria table. "The police are now saying that the person they're looking for doesn't go to FCC. They've checked out everyone who matched the sketch."

Cassandra leaned forward and dropped her voice. "Has anyone heard anything about Courtney and Adam hooking up behind Lucy's back? Lindsey Sloane saw them together in his car a few weeks ago."

Jen turned to me. "You're Courtney's best friend. What about it?" There was something insistent, slightly hostile, and demanding in her voice. It was part of the change at our lunch table that

I'd been noticing. Lucy had always been the focal point. It was a round table, and yet it always felt like Lucy sat at the head. With Courtney and Lucy gone, Jen not only sensed an opportunity to seize control of the group, but for some reason she imagined that I was standing in her way.

"I, um . . ." I fumbled for a moment, not sure how to answer. That was all Jen needed.

"O-M-G!" she gasped. "It's true!"

Suddenly every girl at the table was looking at me. "Tell us," Tabitha urged.

But I had no intention of doing that. "I really don't think we should be talking like this right now."

Jen rolled her eyes dismissively. "Maybe the three of them ran away together. They each waited so it wouldn't look like it was planned."

It was a ridiculous idea, but I kept my mouth shut. There was no reason in the world why all three of them would run away together.

"Or maybe," Cassy said with a glint in her eye, "Adam and Courtney did Lucy in, or something really juicy like that. And they'll make a TV movie of it."

I was tempted to point out that her suggestion wasn't only not funny but totally inappropriate. But Jen glanced expectantly at me and I realized that was exactly what she expected me to do. There was something creepy and disturbing about the undercurrents swirling around the table.

"Oh, and listen to what I heard," said Tabitha. "You know how they had to take Maura away in an ambulance last week? Know why she fainted? She was high on ketamine."

"Horse tranquilizer?" Cassy gasped.

"No way," Jen said dismissively.

"Yes way. My mom's a radiologist at the hospital and one of her best friends works in the ER. She says they get kids coming in high on that stuff all the time." Tabitha leaned closer and dropped her voice even more. "You know where I bet she got it? Sharon. I hear she steals it from her father's office and sells it."

"Why?" Jen asked. "I mean, her father's a vet. It's not like she needs the money."

"She once told me that as soon as high school's over she's moving to San Francisco," Tabitha said. "I guess she wants to save up."

"That's perfect," Cassy chimed in. "I mean, what would you expect? She and her girlfriend. It's so gross."

I'd had enough of their cattiness and gossip. There'd been gossip when Lucy was the queen of this table, but it had never been this nasty. I started to get up.

"Where are you going?" Jen demanded.

I stared straight back to let her know that I didn't appreciate this treatment. "The girls' room. Do I need a pass?"

Inside the girls' room the scent of stale smoke hung in the air; someone had probably sneaked a cigarette a period or two earlier. I looked at myself in the mirror. The rings under my eyes were showing. But it was hard to imagine that anyone at school was sleeping well these days.

A toilet in a stall behind me flushed. The door opened and Sharon stepped out. She hesitated for a second when she saw me in the mirror, then stepped forward and washed her hands.

I hated situations like this, where two people who knew each other were suddenly thrown together with nothing to say.

"So how are you?" I finally asked. "I mean, you know, given everything that's been going on."

"You *really* want to know?" she replied, and, of course, the moment those words left her lips, I realized I probably *didn't* want to know. But it was too late. "For a while I thought it was great. I thought that whoever was doing it, singling out people like your friends, was doing the world a favor."

I stared at her in the mirror, surprised.

"Not what you expected, right?" Sharon said.

She seemed to be letting her guard down. Something I'd never seen her do before. "Can I ask what changed?"

She sighed. "It doesn't matter."

"Maybe deep down you realized that once you get past the cliquishness, they're human beings just like everyone else? That they're not evil and they never did anything to intentionally hurt anyone?"

The lines between her eyes deepened. "Lucy never intentionally hurt you? She didn't steal your boyfriend?"

That was the oldest piece of gossip in the world. Or, at least, in my world. "Adam was never my boyfriend. He was . . . *is* my friend. That's all we ever were. I don't know where that rumor started, but it's not true now and never was."

Sharon gazed steadily at me in the mirror.

"I heard a rumor that you're planning to move to San Francisco after graduation," I said.

She stared down at the sink, shook her head, and blinked hard. I'd never seen her so vulnerable, as if all her defenses had been stripped away. "I was, but . . . forget it."

"Hey, listen," I said. "There's something I need to ask you. I know this is the totally wrong time, but it's important."

She looked at me in the mirror again. "What?"

"Do you know what halothane is?" I asked.

Her expression changed. "It's an anesthetic."

"I heard that the police have been asking people about it. And since your father's a vet?"

She nodded. "They asked him. A detective came to our house."

"Did he say why?"

"I wasn't there," she said. "My dad told me later. . . . Listen, Madison, I know I've been a real bitch, but you don't know what it's like, okay? Anyway, you want to know the truth? I really do hope they're okay." She went past me and out the bathroom door.

I stared at the door, feeling amazed. What in the world could have brought that on?

A moment later I left the girls' room. Lunch wasn't over yet, but I didn't feel like going back to the cafeteria. I stood in the hall for a moment, not sure where to go. The Safe Rides office, I thought, to see if I'd left my red cashmere scarf there on Saturday night.

I pushed open the door, expecting the lights to be off, and was surprised that they were on. A drawer banged shut. Tyler was sitting at the desk, trying not to look rattled.

"Hi," I said uncertainly, not knowing what to think. My emotions were a jumble of conflicting impulses. Should I ask him what he'd been doing? Should I ask why he walked away from me in the hall that morning? Or should I place my hand on his and move close, hoping he'd kiss me the way he had at my house?

"Hi," he replied. We stared at each other. He had to know

that I knew he'd been up to something. I waited. When Tyler looked away, I knew he wasn't going to tell me. Suddenly my feelings focused into anger. He had no right to keep secrets at a time like this. I reached past him and opened the desk drawer. Inside was the Safe Rides log.

"That's what you were looking at," I said, more as a statement than a question.

"Madison, I told you—"

"No!" I cut him short. "People's lives are at stake. If you really know what's going on, you have to tell the police."

He didn't answer. I took out the ring binder and opened it on the desk. "You're thinking that all three of them had something to do with Safe Rides. Lucy disappeared after we gave her that ride home. Adam vanished after he called for a ride. And Courtney was part of Safe Rides."

Tyler eased out of the chair and stood up.

"Why won't you tell the police what you know?" I asked. "Or at least, if *you* won't tell them, tell me and I'll go tell them."

"I better go." He started for the door, but I blocked his path. He looked startled.

"I want you to tell me why you were looking in the log."

We locked eyes. For that one moment I wasn't thinking about how attractive and alluring he was. I just wanted to know what was going on.

"I was looking for a pattern. Something the killer's been following."

I felt a chill. "Who said there was a killer? Who said anyone's been killed?"

Tyler stared at the open log. If there was a killer, and if there was some connection to Safe Rides, it might just be that the killer took his ideas for victims from that log. The log I'd just found Tyler looking at. The same Tyler who, along with me, was the only person in the world who knew that Lucy had not gone inside the night we dropped her off. The same Tyler who'd suddenly said he was going away the weekend Adam disappeared. Only he wasn't away because I'd seen him. The same Tyler who had an unusual interest in serial killers.

"Why are you looking at me like that?" he asked, crashing through my thoughts.

You know nothing about him, I thought. *Not where he came from, or why he suddenly showed up a month after school started, or what he was doing in this office. Do you even want to be in here alone with him?*

I started toward the door.

"You know what it means if they're all dead, don't you?" he asked behind me. "It means that the person who killed them isn't just a killer. He's a serial killer."

On the nights when the public library was open late, Maura used their computers. Her mother had a computer at home, but it had an old-fashioned dial-up modem and you could grow old waiting for it to do the simplest things.

The library was where she had written and posted her blog. And even though she'd stopped doing that, she would still go to a chat room and talk to strangers. And it was there that IaMnEm-EsIs found her.

IaMnEmEsIs: **Do you really think you can just stop?**

The air left Maura's lungs. She stared at the screen, then instinctively looked over her shoulder to see if anyone was watching. No one was. She began to feel anxious and tingly, as if a mild electric current was running through her. She typed:

Str-S-d: **You're the one who has to stop**
IaMnEmEsIs: **Don't tell us what to do. You're in this with us**
Str-S-d: **No**
IaMnEmEsIs: **Who'll believe you?**
Str-S-d: **All I did was write a blog. I didn't know**
IaMnEmEsIs: **You're an accomplice**
Str-S-d: **No!!!!!!!!!!!!!!!!!!!!!!!!!!!!!**
IaMnEmEsIs: **We thought you'd be pleased**
Str-S-d: **You're crazy**
IaMnEmEsIs: **Now there's an original thought**
Str-S-d: **Why did you do it?**
IaMnEmEsIs: **We think you know**
Str-S-d: **Oh, God!!!!!!!!!!!!!!!!!!!**
IaMnEmEsIs: **Too late. We want you to see**
Str-S-d: **See what?**
IaMnEmEsIs: **What we've done for you**
Str-S-d: **No**
IaMnEmEsIs: **Yes. Hillsdale Kennels**
Str-S-d: **Never**
IaMnEmEsIs: **Yes**
Str-S-d: **I'll tell the police**
IaMnEmEsIs: **Can you spell accomplice?**
Str-S-d: **I dont care. I'm not coming**
IaMnEmEsIs: **Then we'll bring it to you**

Maura closed the application. Her heart was pounding.

chapter 19

Wednesday 7:58 A.M.

Don't be upset, Adam. We told Courtney to stop
screaming. We only did what we did because she
wouldn't stop. Why was she screaming? Because of
Lucy, you say? Let's see. Oh, dear, look at that. She
doesn't look well at all, does she? Yes, yes, Adam, it
was just a joke. We know that she's far beyond not
well. We're afraid you're right. Isn't that sad? She had
so much to live for, didn't she? What? What will we do
with her now? Oh, aren't you sweet to be concerned?
Don't worry, Adam. We'll take very good care of her.
The timing couldn't be better.

* * *

IT WAS THE coldest morning so far that fall. A few white flakes drifted out of the gray sky. I had just gotten out of my car in the student parking lot when I heard a scream. Kids all over the lot turned and looked. A few began to jog toward a small patch of trees at the bottom of a short slope next to the school. Others walked slowly toward the trees, as if they wanted to let the runners get there first. Still others, myself included, didn't want to go, or look, or know.

Looking down at the trees I felt a shiver of fear. *Now what?*

A boy named Tanner Wilks ran up the slope as fast as he could. With terror in his eyes he raced past me, yanked open a door that led into the gym, and disappeared inside. Meanwhile, voices, gasps, and shouts came from the wooded area. A girl trudged up the slope sobbing, her face buried in her hands, her shoulder cradled by a grim-looking boy.

The gym door opened and Mr. Alvarez, the gym teacher, raced down the slope towards the woods. The door had hardly closed when it swung open again and Principal Edwards came out, speaking urgently into a walkie talkie as he ran.

"Everyone back! Get back!" Mr. Alvarez's booming gym-teacher voice echoed up the slope. Now Mr. Edwards joined in the chorus. "Everyone go! Get away from here! Go inside. Now!"

A few male teachers went down toward the trees. A small group of female teachers and secretaries came out but stayed near the gym door and watched.

In the distance the police sirens started. Even though they sounded far away, I turned to look and found Tyler standing a few feet behind me. I gasped and felt startled.

He frowned. "I didn't mean to scare you."

"Sorry, I'm just freaked."

"What's going on?" He looked somber as he glanced past me toward the trees.

I shook my head. I didn't know. The sirens were getting louder. I counted two, maybe three different ones, and felt a terrible sensation of foreboding. Tyler stepped closer and I felt his arm go around my shoulders. I shivered and hoped he'd assume it was from the cold, but the truth was, I didn't know how I felt. Yes, I wanted to feel his arm around me, but only if that arm was attached to someone who had nothing to do with the terrible things that were going on. And right now I wasn't sure of that.

A police car screeched into the parking lot. Two officers got out and quickly jogged down the slope and into the woods. An ambulance arrived next, and some EMTs carrying orange medical cases ran down the slope. A dark green sedan pulled into the parking lot, and Detective Payne got out. Our eyes met for a second, and then he hurried down the slope.

Mr. Alvarez and Principal Edwards came out of the woods, both grim and ashen-faced. In a voice filled with angst Principal Edwards shouted, "Everyone, back into school!" In response, kids moved faster toward the doors than they might normally have. Down in the wooded area, a police officer was going from tree to tree, stretching yellow crime-scene tape.

My stomach was in knots and I began to feel light-headed and sick.

"You okay?" Tyler asked.

I nodded but stumbled when I took a step. Tyler slid his arm around my waist. I couldn't tell him that part of my discomfort stemmed from not knowing if I could trust him.

Inside, the PA blared, "Students, go directly to your homerooms and take your seats. Do not congregate in the halls. Go to your homerooms and wait."

The hallways were filled with frightened-looking students. Everyone wanted to know what was going on. Tyler and I passed the nurse's office just as Mrs. Johnson, the school psychologist, rushed in. Through the doorway we could see Tanner Wilks sitting on a cot with his hands over his eyes and Ms. Perkins, the nurse, sitting beside him with her arm around his shoulders.

"What's going on?" I asked.

"It's obvious," Tyler muttered as we continued down the hall.

"But we don't know. I mean, obviously it's something bad, but we don't know."

"The only thing we don't know is which one."

"Please don't say that." At the same time I thought, *One, or ones? If it is them, how does he know it's not all three?*

The thoughts only made me more uncomfortable. I wished he'd take his arm from around my waist. Thank God we were in a crowded hallway at school. I was so uncomfortable with him at that moment that if we'd been someplace else alone, I think I might have screamed and run away.

I was glad when we stopped outside my homeroom. I eased myself out of his grasp. "Guess I better go in."

"Talk to you later?" Tyler asked.

I nodded, but inside I wasn't so sure.

Inside the room Ms. Skelling was sitting quietly at her desk, staring out the window. At their desks, kids were talking anxiously about what was going on outside. Over the PA came the static that often preceded an announcement. "Quiet!" Ms. Skelling suddenly snapped. "Listen!"

"Please pay close attention." Principal Edwards's voice came over the PA. "School has been cancelled for the remainder of the day. If you have a cell phone and can reach a parent or caregiver, please call them and have them come to school to get you. After you've placed your call, please allow someone who doesn't have a phone to use yours. Parents and caregivers are to come as soon as possible. No one will be allowed to leave school alone, even if you came by bicycle or walked this morning. This order has come directly from the chief of police. Teachers, we are depending on you to make sure no student leaves unless accompanied by an adult. Students, if you cannot reach a parent or caregiver, please remain in your homeroom until further notice."

The PA clicked off. There was a moment of silence, as if no one could quite believe we'd been told to use our phones in school, and then kids began calling. I got Mom on her cell. "You have to come get me."

"What's wrong?" she asked. "Are you sick?"

I explained that something bad had happened and that school been cancelled. Mom was silent for a moment. Then she said, "I'll be there as soon as I can."

It wasn't long before a line of cars was snaking into the school driveway and kids were being called over the PA. "Carley Apple-gate, Jason Prine, James Row, Lacey Williamson. Your rides are here. Students who have not been able to reach parents or caregivers, go to the auditorium. Stuart Davies, Melissa Sloat, Randal Ellison, Benjamin Carlucci, please meet your rides."

We watched silently as the kids whose names were called rose and left the classroom.

Tabitha raised her hand. "Can I go to the bathroom?"

"No," said Ms. Skelling.

"But I have to go," Tabitha insisted.

Ms. Skelling rolled her eyes. "Maura, please accompany Tabitha to the young ladies' room and make sure she doesn't go anywhere else and comes right back."

"I don't need a chaperone."

"If you don't like it, you can sit there and pee in your pants," Ms. Skelling said.

Murmurs rippled through the classroom. While Tabitha and Maura got up and left, the rest of us exchanged glances. We weren't used to teachers speaking to us that way, least of all Ms. Skelling. But some in the class suddenly saw an entertaining opportunity to make the time pass.

"What do you think's going on, Ms. Skelling?"

"You'll know soon enough," she replied.

"You think it has something to do with the missing kids?"

"You'll know soon enough."

"You think there's a killer going around killing kids?"

"You'll know . . . soon . . . enough," Ms. Skelling grumbled through clenched teeth. "No . . . more . . . questions."

Another list of names was announced over the PA and mine was among them.

Outside in front of school, Mom was waiting in her car. Her eyes were red and watery. The radio was on: ". . . Miss Cunningham, a senior at Soundview High, was first reported missing on November second. Two other Soundview High students are still missing. This morning's chilling development greatly increases the concern for their lives. . . ."

Using one hand to wipe her eyes, Mom turned off the radio with the other. Tears welled up and spill out of my eyes. *It had happened . . . the worst thing imaginable.*

She drove out of the school driveway and parked on the street, then undid her seat belt and leaned over, doing her best to hug me while I cried.

"I'm so sorry, hon. This is just a terrible thing for someone your age to have to deal with. It's terrible thing for *anyone* to have to deal with. And when I think about Paul and Dana . . ." She didn't finish the sentence. Instead I heard her choke up and start to cry again.

Alternating between wanting to cry and not wanting to, I sobbed, hiccupped, and blew my nose, then cried some more. *This morning's chilling development* . . . Lucy was dead. My friend. Someone my own age. Someone I'd grown up with. Someone I knew . . . had been murdered.

If you've never known someone your own age who's died, you can't imagine what it feels like. It's as if you were walking on a glass floor and it suddenly shatters and now you're falling and falling and there's broken glass in the air all around you and no bottom in sight.

I sat with Mom in the car and cried for a long time. Soon I

wasn't just crying for Lucy, but for Adam and Courtney as well. Were they also dead?

"How can this be happening?" I sobbed.

Mom wiped her eyes and shook her head. "I don't know, hon. I've never experienced anything like this before. I've never *heard* of anything like this before."

Rap! Rap! The sound of knuckles on the window made us jump. Mom and I swiveled our heads. A woman with straight black hair was gesturing for me to open the window. She was holding a microphone, and behind her was a man with a video camera.

"Cover your face and put up your middle finger," Mom said.

"What?!" I asked in disbelief.

"Just do it," she said. "Then they can't use it on air."

I did as I was told. The reporter and cameraman left. I turned to Mom. My eyes burned and my cheeks were wet, but I felt a smile on my lips. "God, Mom, I never thought the day would come when *you'd* tell me to give someone the finger."

We shared a brief grin that quickly dissolved into more tears. My grandmother had died of cancer, and in third grade a girl in the year ahead of me had died suddenly from an asthma attack. But this was different. This was . . . murder. Something that only happened in movies and on TV, and in places far away. Something that no one ever imagined happening in a place like Soundview.

I spent the rest of the day at home, texting, talking, IMing, and thinking about Tyler. He wasn't online, but he was there in my head, gnawing at my thoughts. I didn't want to believe he was involved in Lucy's death, but I couldn't be sure he wasn't.

And then there were the tears, which were never far away as the whole reality of Lucy's death hit me again and again. Each time I finished crying, I'd go downstairs and find Mom on *her* computer and phone, and we'd go into the kitchen and make tea. Dad was in London, but Mom reached him and he left a dinner with some important people to speak to me for a while. The TV stayed off. Mom said we'd had enough bad news for one day (although I had a feeling she was checking the news while I was upstairs).

I was sitting in the kitchen, gazing at the Sound. The water was steel gray, reflecting the sky. The breeze drove row after row of small waves across the surface, but all I could think about was the cold, still darkness beneath.

"Honey?" Mom asked.

"Yes?" I raised my head.

Mom smiled crookedly as she came toward me with a jar of honey in her hand. "I meant, for your tea."

"Oh, sure, thanks." She set the jar down and I transferred a spoonful of the amber syrup into my mug. The phone rang and Mom answered. "Yes? Uh-huh. Yes, I understand. I'll tell her." She hung up. "No school tomorrow."

That didn't come as a surprise. Everyone was beyond freaked. School the next day would have been a waste, and there was a good chance a lot of parents would keep their kids home anyway. Mom sat down and cupped her hands around her mug. "I guess what I'm wondering is how in the world they're going to have school the day *after* tomorrow?"

* * *

When I went back upstairs there was a message from PBleeker:

> I guess you must be pretty upset, unless maybe you're
> happy about what happened because Lucy stole Adam from
> you. But people don't deserve to die just because they steal
> someone's boyfriend, do they? Besides, you've never struck
> me as the vengeful type. Can you believe what they did to
> her eyes?

The first rule of dealing with cyberstalkers is to never, ever respond. But this felt different. Even if I wasn't sure who PBleeker was, it was obvious that we knew each other. I wrote back: *What about her eyes?*

I waited, hoping that PBleeker would be thrilled that I'd finally answered, and eager to reply. But no reply came.

That night there was more news about Lucy. The medical examiner announced that she'd been dead for less than twenty-four hours when she'd been discovered in that wooded grove near the school that morning. The cause of death appeared to be kidney failure due to severe dehydration. There was no mention of anything relating to eyes.

chapter 20

Thursday 6:43 A.M.

NORMALLY WHEN I got up in the morning, Mom was already downstairs with the newspaper. She read the paper daily, not only because she was active in town politics but because she was a news junkie. But the following morning there was no paper spread out on the kitchen table. There was only Mom, wearing her white terry-cloth robe, the ends of her hair still damp from a morning swim. She was gazing out the window. When she heard me come in, she turned and gave me a weak smile. "How'd you sleep?"

"Better than I thought I would," I said. "I guess massive anxiety can really wear you out." I sat down and poured myself a mug of tea. "What's up?"

"Just having my coffee." That was so un-Mom-like.

"Why aren't you reading the paper?"

She gave me a completely unconvincing shrug.

"Mom, I already heard."

She reached across the table and placed her hand on mine. "About how she died?"

I nodded, although trying to make sense of what they'd said was like trudging through heavy snow. *Kidney failure . . . dehydration . . .*

Mom must have seen that I was struggling. "They think . . . it means that wherever she was she couldn't get anything to drink."

"Why not?"

Mom blinked and her eyes got watery. "I don't think anyone really knows. But if I had to guess, the answer would be that someone didn't want her to drink." Tears began to run down her cheeks.

I was usually such a homebody, but for once it was hard to stay inside. Maybe it was the craziness of what was going on. Maybe it was my yearning to sort out things with Tyler. Whatever it was, it was impossible to stay still. There was nothing good on TV and I didn't want to sit at the computer all day exchanging IMs based on gossip and rumors. I tried to read, but that didn't work, either. Nothing did.

I was paging through a *Seventeen* magazine when Mom knocked on my door and came in wearing business clothes. "There's a board of directors meeting at the hospital. I hate to leave you, but I know you'll be safe here. Is that okay?"

I didn't want her to go, but she was right. It was hard to imagine anyplace safer than my own house, in the gated community of Premium Point, in the (formerly) ultra-safe suburb of Soundview. "It's okay, Mom. How long do you think you'll be?"

"They usually go for most of the afternoon. Some people just love the sound of their own voices." She came over and kissed me on the head. "You'll be okay. I'll keep my cell phone on."

"No prob, Mom."

She left and I wished she hadn't gone. It wasn't logical; I just didn't want to be alone in the house. Not today. Who could I invite over? Tyler was the only one who came to mind, and I didn't feel comfortable calling him.

I finished looking at the magazine. The house was empty, and my room began to feel claustrophobic in my room. I went downstairs and walked around, making sure all the doors were locked and the windows were shut. I would have turned on the alarm system, but it was wired to first-floor motion detectors and that meant having to stay upstairs to avoid setting them off.

There were coffee-table books in the living room to look at and more magazines in the kitchen to read. And there was always the Sound to gaze at, but I'd done a lot of that lately. I couldn't sit still. Every time I did, thoughts I didn't want to have were quick to appear. What did it feel like to die of dehydration? What did someone who'd died from dehydration look like? If Lucy hadn't been given anything to drink, was the same true of Adam and Courtney?

And of course, there was Tyler. Tyler, Tyler, Tyler, until I felt like I'd go crazy.

I went upstairs and changed into exercise clothes, then jogged on the treadmill while watching *Ten Things I Hate About You*, one of my favorite movies. That worked for a while, until I got tired and had to slow from a jog to a walk, and then — when my legs really began to ache — to a stop altogether. But at least I knew what I wanted to do next.

The indoor-outdoor pool and hot tub were separated from the house by a long, narrow breezeway lined with sliding-glass doors. In summer we opened the doors and retracted the pool's roof. In the winter the doors were closed and the roof went back on. I guess the indoor hot tub was what people would call a guilty pleasure. I loved sitting in it after exercising or riding Val, with the bubbling hot water swirling around me and the view of the Sound out back. As I walked along the breezeway, I saw that the blue sky was dotted with high thin clouds as wispy as baby's hair and the sun sparkled on the water. But in the distance to the west, a thick bank of dark gray clouds was approaching.

The hot tub was in a corner between the pool and the windows. I turned the whirlpool on and waited for the water to heat up. It hardly took any time for the hot tub to get steamy. I took off my white terry-cloth robe and draped it over a pool chair. I was naked. It seemed silly to bother with a bathing suit when there was absolutely no one around. Before I got into the tub, goose bumps ran over my skin, more from the daring thrill of being completely unclothed than any lingering cool air.

I eased myself into the bubbly brew and immediately felt myself start to relax. The windows closest to the hot tub steamed over and I stared at the ceiling, trying to let my mind go anywhere it wanted as long as it had nothing to do with Lucy, Adam, and Courtney. Or Tyler.

There was college to think about. But then I imagined what the first day would be like. I'd meet other students and they'd ask where I was from and as soon as I said Soundview they were sure to press their hands to their mouths and gasp, "Isn't that where those kids disappeared and that girl was killed?"

The thought made me wince. Would this follow all of us for the rest of our lives? Would we always be the kids from Soundview—like the kids who went to Columbine?

I slid down a little in the hot tub and let the swirling bubbly water cover my shoulders. And thought about Tyler again. *Okay, okay,* I thought. *I give up. As soon as I get out, I'll call him. Either I'll make up some excuse, or I'll just tell him the truth . . . that I would feel better if he told me more about himself and what was going on.*

That's what I was thinking when I looked back at the window . . . and felt a jolt of terror. Against the foggy glass was a shadow—a silhouette of someone, almost certainly a man.

My breath grew short and my heart banged in my chest. Who was he and what was he doing there? It could have been a gardener or one of the workmen Mom sometimes hired to do chores around the house. But he wasn't carrying a rake or any tools. The shadow's arm rose and a hand pressed against the glass as if he were trying to peer in, but the vapor was on the inside and he couldn't wipe it away. I stayed in the hot tub, frozen with fear. If I kept perfectly still, maybe he wouldn't see me.

The man began to walk along the sliding doors. The vapor fogging the windows didn't extend very far. Soon he'd reach clear glass and be able to see in. I looked at the terry-cloth robe on the pool chair. Did I have time to get out of the hot tub and put it on?

No. He reached a pane of clear glass and peered in at the pool, his head slowly turning in the direction of the hot tub. Even before his eyes met mine, I thought I recognized him. The wavy hair and the chipped tooth. He was the person of interest. The one in the sketch Reilly had given the police. Only his face was covered by a short beard and his hair was longer than in the sketch, and uncombed.

I still hadn't moved when our eyes met. For a second he actually looked startled to see me. Then his hand went to the sliding door's handle, but it was locked from the inside. He moved to the next door and tried that, but it was also locked. He looked up and our eyes met again. He gestured with his hand for me to come and open the door from the inside.

I was frozen with fear, my stomach knotting, my chest so tight I could hardly breathe. All I could think about was getting back into the house to call for help. I looked again at the robe on the chair. His eyes followed mine and he blinked as if he knew what I was thinking. He moved down to the next sliding door and tried it. And then the next.

I was almost sure all the sliding doors were locked. Once we closed them for the winter, we never went through them. But he didn't know that. He moved farther away along the outside of the breezeway, down to the next sliding door. What would he do once he realized all the doors were locked? I didn't know, but I did know that I couldn't stay in the hot tub any longer. But if I got out, he would see me. Naked.

He reached the last sliding door and tried it, but like the others, it wouldn't open. Terrified, I watched as he looked around, up, and down, as if trying to find a way to get in. *He's not going to stop*, I thought. *He's going to keep trying until he gets in. He knows he can't just go away because I've seen him and he knows I'll call the police. He killed Lucy. He may have killed Adam and Courtney, as well. He's not going to just change his mind and go away.*

I got out of the hot tub, covering myself with my hands as best as I could, and quickly pulled on the robe. He saw me and started back along the windows. But now I wouldn't look at him. Keeping him in the corner of my eye, I hurried along the side of the pool, toward the breezeway.

He stopped by a sliding door as if he thought I was going to open it for him. I couldn't imagine why he would think that, and I didn't care. When I didn't stop to let him in, he scowled and began to jog alongside me on the other side of the glass.

"Let me in!" he yelled. "I have to talk to you."

I started to run toward the breezeway. I had to get into the house. There was a panic button by the front door. I would trip it, then lock myself in a bathroom.

"You have to listen to me!" he yelled, still moving alongside me.

What I had to do was get to a phone and call the police. I started toward the house. Outside, the man raced ahead, trying the sliding doors that lined the breezeway. "I have to talk to you!"

Forget the panic button, I thought. *Just get to the phone. Call the police. Then lock yourself in a bathroom.*

"Wait!" He thumped his hand against the glass.

I kept going. Up ahead, near where the breezeway met the house, someone had left a wheelbarrow and a shovel outside. The man stopped and picked up the shovel. I kept running.

Crash! Glass shattered behind me.

Get to the phone, I told myself as I ran. *You have to get to the phone.*

I went through the door at the end of the breezeway and into the exercise room, past the treadmill and stationary bike. From behind me came grunting and the clatter of broken glass falling to the floor.

He'd gotten in.

The next room was the kitchen.

Get to the phone. Dial 911.

I got into the kitchen, grabbed the phone, and turned the keypad to face me. I could hear footsteps and heavy breathing coming closer. I jabbed my finger down. 9 . . . 1 . . .

The phone was ripped from my hand, and clattered to the floor. I felt his hands close tight around my arms, and looked up into his face. It was dirty, the beard untrimmed, his hair wild. He smelled of sour sweat. "You have to listen—"

I could hardly breathe from fear. My heart was speeding, my whole body shaking. My stomach felt like a rubber band twisted a thousand times. I knew what I was supposed to do. *Kick him*, I thought. *Do it!*

But I'd never kicked anybody on purpose. I'd never even hit anyone. I knew it was okay. There was nothing wrong with it. It was exactly what I was supposed to do. What my parents would want me to do.

"Listen to me!" he demanded.

I shook my head and tried to twist out of his grasp, but it was no use. He was squeezing my arm so tight it hurt.

"Stop fighting!" he said.

Kick him, I thought. *Do it!*

"Listen!"

I stopped struggling. I was terrified, and dizzy. My head felt light. Everything began to spin. The floor was racing up toward me.

When my eyes opened, I was lying on my back. The lights in the kitchen ceiling were off. Something cold and wet was on my forehead. I could hear crunching. I propped myself up on one elbow. The man was sitting on the floor beside me, eating a bowl of granola. A little white ribbon of milk trickled down his beard.

"You okay?" he asked, chewing.

I slid the wet dishtowel off my forehead and sat up. My robe was pulled down past my knees, as if he had arranged it to cover as much as possible. With one hand I pinched the collar tight around my neck. Somehow I knew he hadn't touched me. Still, even with the robe on, I could feel my nakedness beneath. I looked around. Where was the phone?

"Don't worry," he said, and swallowed. "I'm not going to hurt you."

Was he saying that to get me to drop my guard? If he didn't want to hurt me, why had he broken in? I wished I had more clothes on and wasn't trembling so much. After swallowing to moisten my throat, I asked, "What are you doing here? What do you want with me?"

Instead of answering, he shoved another spoonful of granola into his mouth and chewed. "You can't believe how hungry I am," he said, his cheeks bulging.

You shouldn't talk with your mouth full, I thought nervously.

He swallowed. "The cops are looking for me. Your friend Tyler is looking for me. They all think I killed Megan."

"Megan Woodworth?"

He nodded. "Tyler told you?"

"No, someone e-mailed me a newspaper article," I said. I'd also once read an article about a woman who'd been kidnapped and had spent hours talking calmly to the kidnapper until he let her go. But was that kidnapper a granola-eating serial killer?

He nodded and shoveled another spoonful between his lips. "Megan was my girlfriend."

"Why is Tyler looking for you?" I asked.

He stopped chewing. "He didn't tell you?"

I shook my head.

"Megan's his sister."

"But his last name is Starling and I thought her last name was Woodworth."

"Starling?" He stared up at the kitchen ceiling as if thinking. "Oh, I get it. Clarice Starling."

"Who?"

"The Jodie Foster character in *Silence of the Lambs*," he said. "Tyler's convinced himself that I'm a serial killer."

"You're not?"

He leveled his gaze at me and smiled slightly. "Do I strike you as a serial killer?"

He didn't. He sounded like a reasonable, intelligent, hungry, dirty, smelly person. Was it possible that he was some kind of psychopath? One of those people you read about who acts perfectly normal and then goes out and kills people? And all the neighbors say he was such a nice, quiet man who wouldn't hurt a fly?

"Do you have a name?" I asked.

"Ethan Landers."

"And you're on the run?"

He smirked. "Whatever gave you that idea?"

I realized I could add "sense of humor" to his description. No, he didn't seem like a psychopath at all.

"Why don't you just go to the police and tell them the truth?" I asked.

"You mean, go to them and say, 'Hey, guys, despite the evidence you have against me, I'm really innocent'? Now there's a novel idea. Wonder if it's ever been tried before?" The words seethed with ironic bitterness. "I was set up to make it look like I killed Megan. You can't believe something like that could actually happen in real life, and then it does and it's just uncomprehendable. And maybe the police don't have all the evidence against me that they'd like to have, but they have enough to charge me and make me stand trial. And then I either have to hire an experienced lawyer, which costs a fortune and there's no way I can afford it, or I have to put my fate in the hands of some overworked, inexperienced public defender. Think about it. Your entire life in the hands of some guy or girl who just got out of law school six months ago, has way more cases than he can possibly handle, probably little or no experience with murder cases, and he's supposed to defend you for a killing you didn't even commit? It's like something out of Kafka. Would you take that chance?"

I shook my head. He sounded as rational and logical as anyone I knew.

"Yeah, well, neither would I," he said. "Running from the law is probably the stupidest thing I've ever done, but at least I feel like my fate is in my hands. At least this way I have a chance to prove I'm innocent and show them what's really going on."

"And what is really going on?"

He told me.

* * *

Ethan was the one whose footsteps I'd heard in the boatyard, where he'd been hiding in the dry-docked boats ever since he'd arrived in Soundview. It was he who'd left the notes and slashed my tires. He'd done it to make sure I didn't go to Courtney's the night she'd had that get-together. He was worried that something bad might happen to me.

"Why me?"

"I'd heard about you. You sounded like my best chance at finding someone I could trust. I need someone on the inside. Someone who knows everyone and can tell me what's going on."

It all sounded logical and plausible. Why do we believe one stranger and not another? I wondered. What made me think I was smart enough to tell the difference between honesty and a well-disguised lie? Could I take that chance?

He seemed to know what I was thinking. "Give me ten minutes on your computer, okay? Let me show you what I know. Then you can decide for yourself what to do."

To let him use my computer would mean letting him into my bedroom, and I didn't want to do that. "You can use my mom's." I pointed at the laptop in her office beside the kitchen.

Ethan sat down. I stood behind him. Now that he'd been inside for a while and had warmed up, the sour scent of his body odor was even stronger.

"Have you heard about any break-ins at veterinary clinics around here?" he asked as he searched for sites.

"The police have been asking veterinarians about halothane. And it was mentioned in the newspaper story I read."

"That's what she uses to knock out her victims. Any news

about people finding animals with their eyes gouged out?"

The thought was revolting. But not as horrible as the realization that followed. "Oh my God!"

Ethan looked quizzically over his shoulder at me. I had to sit down. My stomach turned inside out and I crossed my arms and doubled over. *Lucy! Oh, no! Oh, God! How awful! How unbearably horrible!*

"You okay?" Ethan asked.

"There's this person who sends me anonymous messages," I said. "I don't know if it's a guy or a girl. The last message I got asked if I could believe what they did to my friend's eyes. The one they found near school. I didn't know what that meant."

Ethan nodded grimly. "I'm sorry."

My eyes teared up and I squeezed them shut. *Will it ever stop?* I wondered. *Or will each day bring some new, more horrible news?*

"I don't know if you want to read this." He pointed at the computer screen. I stood up and looked. It was an article from the *Shawnee Mission Gazette-Recorder* about a break-in at a veterinary clinic. Then he showed me another story that appeared a few weeks later about some feral cats found by the side of the road with their eyes gouged out and traces of halothane in their systems.

"Wait," I said. "The newspaper article I read about Megan's friend Molly said something about a mutilation, too."

Ethan nodded knowingly. "If you go back and search for instances of break-ins in veterinary clinics, and you match them to stories about finding animals with their eyes gouged out, you'll find matches in Florida, the state of Washington, southern California, and Kansas, where I'm from."

"What about Megan?" I asked.

Ethan shrugged and said sadly, "Who knows? They've never found her."

"Oh, God, this is awful," I said.

Ethan started a new search, talking to me as he typed. "Have you ever heard of Nemesis?"

"It's a word."

"It's also the Greek goddess of revenge," Ethan said. "She's got some kind of connection to it. After Molly disappeared, Megan told me she'd gotten a couple of really strange e-mails from someone calling themselves Nemesis."

Results began to appear in the screen—comments on blogs, but nothing that appeared recognizable.

"Try *Lucy Cunningham* and *Nemesis*," I said.

Ethan typed. Results began to pop up. The word *nemesis* highlighted with someone whose first name was Lucy and someone else whose last name was Cunningham. Things in strange languages. PDF documents. Fragments that made no sense.

Then I saw something scroll past on the screen. "Stop! Go back."

Ethan went back.

Str-S-d #7

about how Lucy Cunningham has disappeared. Some people think Lucy... wish I could make some of the kids around heeere disappeeear.

IaMnEmEsIs said...
People get what they deserve.

Tony2theman said...
Why be sorry?

"What is that?" I asked.

"Looks like a blog." Ethan clicked on the link and a new page appeared:

Str-S-d #1

Today at school Lucy Cunningham looked at me like I was something the cat coughed up. I don't have to explain who Lucy is. You already know, because there's only one kind of girl who would look at anyone that way.

Str-S-d #3

This girl once asked me why I didn't at least wear nicer clothes. That's what she said, "at least." As if it bothered her that I didn't even try. Not that my mom has the money. But that's not the real answer. The real answer is . . .

Str-S-d #5

It's taken me a long time to get to this point. I said I was
being honest in this blog, but I wasn't completely because
I didn't say what I was really thinking. I mean, wishing
people would die. That's how I really feel most of the time.
I just wish they would die. I didn't write it before because
I tell myself I shouldn't feel that way. But the more I try
to rid myself of these thoughts, the stronger they grow.
So forget trying to be nice. Forget trying to pretend. Those
people have made my life miserable. I want them to die.

I'll begin with Lucy. She is definitely first on the list.
You can't believe how it feels to be in the cafeteria and
turn around and there she is staring at me like I'm some
disgusting bug or vermin. Does she really think I WANT to
be this way? I hate you, Lucy. I really hate you. You are my
#1 pick. I wish you were dead.

•••

💬 4 Comments

Realgurl4013 said...
I know just how you feel. Popular kids suuuck.

Ru22cool? said...
Did it ever occur to you to try and improve your looks
instead of just being a crybaby complainer?

Str-S-d said...
Go read Str-S-d #4, Ru22.

IaMnEmEsIs said...
Perhaps your wish will come true.

Ethan turned and looked at me. "Any idea who could have written this?"

"Yes," I said, and kept reading until I got to:

Str-S-d #11

This is the last blog I'm writing. I'm really scared. I wished three people would die, and now they're all gone. I don't believe anymore that it's a coincidence. Someone's been reading this blog. Someone crazy enough to do what I wished for. If you're reading this right now, you know who you are. You're the one person in the world who is always nice to me. But today in school you said something. I'm not sure you even realized what you were saying, but it totally creeped me out. Now I don't know what to do. I could go to the police, but they'll want to know how I know and then they'll find out about this blog and blame me. The parents will blame me. Everyone will blame me. Everyone already hates me. But this is the worst thing that ever happened. Maybe I should kill myself. I could kill myself, but then someone would figure it out. I don't want to be blamed for this. Even if I'm dead.

I actually put my hand on his shoulder and stared at the screen, utterly, totally incredulous. This time Ethan didn't turn around. He just said, "She knows who it is."

I'd told him I had to get dressed and I didn't want him in the house when I did. He said he understood and would wait for me outside. We went to the door.

"You realize I could still call the police?" I said.

His shoulders sagged, and he hung his head and stared at the ground. "Look, I've told you the truth. You read the newspaper stories and saw what was on the Internet. If I were Nemesis, why would I have told you about all that?"

"I don't know," I said. "But you just broke into my house and now you're asking me to trust you."

He sighed and nodded. "You're right. I did that because I'm desperate. I've been on the run for a long time. I'm tired and dirty and smelly, and I feel like the whole world is against me—and if you've never felt that way, believe me, it's hard to keep going. This is the closest I've gotten to Nemesis, but I need help. The person who wrote that blog has no reason to talk to me, but they may talk to you. So here's the deal. You can call the police and I'll be arrested. As soon as Nemesis hears about it, she'll be gone . . . off to some new place and new identity, and sooner or later she'll kill more kids. Or you can trust me and help me stop her once and for all. It's up to you."

He gestured back into the house. "There's the phone." Then he sat down on the front step under the portico. "Either way, I'll be here."

I closed the front door and locked it. By the time I'd gotten back to my room upstairs, I'd made my decision.

Rain splattered on the Audi's windshield. The address was a street I'd never heard of, in a part of town I'd never known anyone to live. A few blocks of old, two-story wood and brick buildings housing a car-repair and body shop, a plumbing-supply store, a small industrial dry cleaner. On the second floors of some of the buildings were apartments. Rainwater dripped from the roofs and awnings. The address was a store that sold and fixed vacuum cleaners. Above it was an apartment. I parked across the street.

"Want me to come with you?" Ethan asked.

"No, I'm afraid it will freak her out."

I left the car and crossed the street in the rain. The paint on the small brown wooden door beside the vacuum-cleaner store was peeling. The door was unlocked. I pushed it open and went in. On the wall of the dark vestibule inside were two metal mailboxes. One said BRESLISS.

I climbed the narrow creaky wooden stairs. The steps were so old they dipped in the middle. On the second-floor landing were some children's bicycles, a stroller, and two doors. I knocked on the one marked BRESLISS.

"Who's there?" a woman shouted from inside.

"My name is Madison Archer," I said to the door. "Is Maura there?"

"What do you want?"

"I'm a friend of hers."

I could hear muttering on the other side of the door. Then the woman said, "That's a first. Go get your sister. Someone's here for her."

I heard banging and yelling, and then the soft slither of footsteps. "Who is it?" Maura asked.

"It's Madison."

Silence. The door didn't open.

"Maura?" I said. There was no answer. "Maura, I know what's going on. I remember what you told me that day in the hall and I read your blog."

"Your what?" the woman inside asked. Obviously she'd been listening.

The door opened just enough for Maura to squeeze out. As if she didn't want me to see inside. I caught a glimpse of the woman. Small, like Maura, with a hard, deeply lined face.

Maura pulled the door closed behind her and then led me back down the stairs. We stood in the small, dark vestibule. "How did you find my blog?" she asked.

"A friend helped me," I said. "You don't know who he is, and he doesn't know who you are, but I can promise you that neither he nor I will ever tell anyone. I swear, and I trust him. You can trust him. But there's one thing we need to know, Maura. We need to know where she is."

"You're sure you want to do this?" I asked nervously as I drove.

"If you're asking if I'm scared, the answer is totally," Ethan replied. "But what choice do I have?"

"Can't we just go to the police?"

He gazed steadily at me. "Look, I know you don't know me and don't have any reason to care about me, but I'm asking you to believe me. I'm begging you. The cops have a sketch. They have an FBI profiler telling them to look for a single male loner. The second you tell the police, I'll be arrested for Molly's murder, and by the time the cops figure out what really happened—*if* they ever figure out what really happened—your other friends will wind up dead."

The address I'd gotten from Maura was in a town I'd never been to before. My GPS said we had twenty-seven minutes to go.

"Your friend Lucy," Ethan said. "Was she popular?"

"Uh-huh."

"And not real nice to kids who weren't?"

"It wasn't her fault."

Ethan shrugged as if it didn't matter.

"Was Megan . . . popular and not very nice?" I asked.

He nodded. "I can make excuses for her. Deep down she was really insecure and driven. But basically, yeah. She could have been nicer."

"And you?"

"What did I know? I was just your typical high-school jock having fun."

We rode a few more miles. The rain seemed to be letting up.

"Why does she do it?" I asked.

"I don't know. I'm not a shrink."

"But you must have an idea. You've been following her, researching, trying to figure it out."

"Okay, here's my theory," he said. "But it's mostly supposition, okay? I think maybe when she was a teenager, it was a seriously bad time for her. She was probably one of those plain, quiet girls—"

"But—" I began.

"Let me finish," he said. "And for whatever reason, she got teased a lot. Stared at. Pushed around. Maybe her family didn't have anything and she got singled out for that. I don't know. I'm just guessing, right? So she grows up thinking someday she's going to change. Become a totally different person. Make enough money to get all the cosmetic work done and be the person she always dreamed of becoming. The face, the breasts, who knows what else? But it doesn't work. Whatever she dreamed would happen doesn't. She changes everything but nothing changes. The dream she's clung to for all these years is dashed. Whatever it was, whatever she waited all this time for, it doesn't come true."

"So she becomes angry, bitter, resentful," I said.

"Worse," said Ethan. "Vindictive, revengeful. Nemesis."

"What about the eyes? The animals?"

"Who knows? She's got that science background. Maybe she tried veterinary school for a while and couldn't cut it. Excuse the unintentional pun. One thing I do know is something a lot of serial killers have in common is animal torture."

"I thought serial killers were always men," I said.

"*Mostly* men," Ethan corrected me. "One out of six is a woman. Aileen Wuornos, Belle Gunness, Marie Noe. Not nearly as common as male serial killers, but not unheard of."

"How did you figure out she was here in Soundview?" I asked.

"Before I left Kansas, I broke into the place where she'd lived while she was there. She'd done a pretty good job of cleaning it out, so there'd been no evidence . . . nothing I could show the police to prove I'd been set up. But I did find a printout of teaching jobs, and an ad for a chemistry teacher at Soundview High School was circled."

We were getting closer. Each turn put us on a narrower, less well-paved, and less populated road, until we were headed up a hill with nothing but bare trees and ground covered with brown, dead leaves. Patches of mist drifted across the road, which was now only wide enough for one car, the asphalt crumbling and dotted with potholes. We came to a narrow gravel driveway that wound back through the trees and disappeared. On a post beside the driveway was a dented mailbox and a small peeling sign that said, HILLSDALE KENNELS.

I slowed the car.

"Keep going," Ethan said.

I drove up the hill about a quarter mile, where the road ended at a driveway leading to the remains of a small dilapidated house. The roof had sunk in and the windows were broken. It was clear that no one had lived there in a long time.

"Okay," Ethan said. "Turn around and go back down. I'll tell you where to park."

About a quarter of a mile back down the road, he pointed at a small clearing. "Pull over here."

I did as I was told.

Ethan sat still for a moment. Then he said, "You don't have to come. It would probably be better if you didn't."

I didn't want to go. I was scared half out of my mind. Heart thudding, stomach twisting. But I felt like I'd spent my whole life being scared. At some point I just had to stop and do something. "They're my friends."

He leveled his gaze at me. "Think about it. I have nothing to lose and everything to gain. You have a lot to lose and not that much to gain."

"Please stop trying to talk me out of this. If you try hard enough, you just may succeed, and I don't want you to."

He raised an eyebrow skeptically but said, "Okay, let's go."

We got out. The air was cold and moist, the kind of chill that creeps through your clothes. The rain had turned into a thick, misty drizzle, and our breaths came out in white vapor. The faint smell of wood smoke was in the air. Someone somewhere had a fire going. Ethan walked along the side of the road, looking to his left, in the direction of the kennel, even though it was invisible beyond the myriad tree trunks. He paused for a moment, then tilted his head toward the woods. We started to walk through the trees, the wet, dead leaves squishing under our feet.

Ethan stepped carefully, avoiding sticks that might crack loudly underfoot, and I did the same. All I could see were bare, dark tree trunks, but the scent of smoke seemed to grow stronger. I don't know how Ethan could know where he was going, unless he was following that scent. I still couldn't quite believe I was follow-ing this stranger—this person who'd broken into my own home, who was on the run from the law—deep into unknown woods. Had I lost my mind? Was I completely insane? And yet somehow I'd come to believe, very quickly, that I could trust him. I'd heard his side of the story. It made sense. Sometimes you had to take a leap of faith. Especially if it might mean saving your friends' lives.

Ethan stopped. Up ahead, barely visible through the wet tree trunks, was a low, dark green house. Smoke curled up from a nar-row cinder-block chimney. Ethan looked back at me and nodded as if to say, *This is it*. He started walking again.

I followed, glancing from his back to the house ahead. As we got closer, I could see a fenced-in enclosure. It could have been an outdoor kennel. There were low, wooden shelters inside— doghouses.

Ethan paused beside a tree. So far there'd been no sign of life or movement around the house. I moved up close behind him and whispered, "What do you think?"

"I think if there are dogs there and they start barking, we're toast," he answered, and gazed past me back in the direction of the road. "You don't have to do this. You can still go back."

"I know," I said.

Our eyes met, and he nodded slightly as if accepting my decision. Then he turned and continued. I could see the fenced-in area now. Something moved quickly back and forth along the fence. A medium-size black dog. Ethan stopped. The dog was excited, as if it knew we were coming. Its tongue hung out and its tail wagged rapidly. Ethan didn't move. I wondered if he was waiting to see if it would bark, or if the dog's excited movements brought someone out of the house.

But nothing changed. The dog kept turning and turning by the fence. Ethan stepped slowly. The low green house looked neglected. A shovel and hayfork leaned against the wall near a door. The roof was missing shingles, and old branches lay on it. Some of the windows were cracked, and most appeared to be covered on the inside with plastic sheeting.

Ethan stopped about ten yards from the fence. The dog paced more frantically than ever, emitting little yelps and cries but not barking. I realized Ethan was staring at the small black box attached to its collar—one of those awful things that sent a shock each time a dog barked.

The kennel was divided into pens, each with its own doghouse. But no other dogs appeared. The foul odor of excrement replaced the scent of burning wood. Ethan took a few steps closer, then stopped again. I could almost feel him stiffen. He was looking at the doghouse in one of the pens. Protruding from the opening were human legs, covered by filthy jeans, ending with dirt-covered bare feet. Male feet.

I felt a gasp burst from my lungs. Ethan heard it and turned quickly, cautioning me with his eyes against making any sounds. Despite my beating heart and churning stomach, I nodded back.

We moved closer. The smell got worse and I could see evidence that the cages hadn't been cleaned out in a long time. The human feet didn't move. Were they Adam's. Was he alive?

We were a few yards from the kennel. Inside were half a dozen pens, each in its own doghouse. The black dog charged back and forth frantically, its tail whipsawing. I got the feeling that it desperately hoped that whoever we were, we would take it away from this place. Meanwhile the legs protruding from the doghouse had yet to move or give any sign of life.

And then I saw something else. The slightest movement through the opening in one of the other doghouses. A face appeared, streaked with dirt and surrounded by long black matted hair streaked with pink and blonde.

I touched Ethan's shoulder and pointed. Courtney cowered inside the doghouse, her eyes wild and darting. There was something square and black strapped to her neck. I lost my breath when I realized what it was—the same thing the dog was wearing. My lungs stopped and my stomach unknotted and reknotted itself more tightly. I fought the urge to turn around and run. *You've come too far. . . .* I caught her eye and gestured for her to come out. Her eyes widened and darted again. Something was scaring her out of her mind.

Crack!

The impact of metal against skull made me jump. Next to me, Ethan collapsed in a loose-limbed heap.

I started to turn when a hand grasped the back of my head. Another came toward my face with a rag. The wet cloth slammed against my nose and mouth. The smell was pungent and sickeningly sweet. I reached up to pull the rag away, but my thoughts were already disappearing into a white cottony cloud. My arms began to feel heavy and I couldn't get my hands to work. My knees went rubbery and I began to fall.

My shoulder throbbed with pain. I opened my eyes and saw chair legs. A rug spread out before me like an ocean. A prairie of silvery dust under the couch. A long, fat green duffel bag lay beside a black garbage bag held closed with a yellow tie. Voices came from somewhere close by.

I lay on my side on the floor, on my aching shoulder, my hands tied tightly behind my back. My ankles were bound and when I tried to straighten my legs, it pulled at my wrists. So I knew my hands and feet were tied together behind me. I could feel something strapped around my neck, and two hard bumps pressing against the bare skin.

The voices were coming from the TV. Some women were discussing the pros and cons of having more than one relationship at a time. One voice sounded familiar. Oprah's. I twisted my head around. There was no one on the couch. The room was empty. The TV was on, but no one was watching.

"She's only saying that because she's on TV," a voice said. But this one wasn't from the TV. It was coming from another room.

"You don't know that."

"Oh, come on, it's so obvious."

"How would you know?"

"You can tell she's just saying it for the shock value. Morons like her will do anything to get on the tube. She doesn't believe a word she's saying."

"You don't know that."

I was listening to a conversation between one person. The same voice speaking both sides of the argument. It was a voice I knew well. I twisted my head around. Where was Ethan? The memory came back of that sickening crack when she hit him on the head.

A bell pinged and I heard a microwave oven open and slam shut, followed by the slither of slippers. They came through a doorway—old, yellow, and terry cloth. I twisted my head higher. Baggy orange sweatpants. A navy blue hoodie. A tray with some sort of steaming food in a black plastic bowl. Thick red hair. The slippers stopped. Ms. Skelling looked down at me. She made a face but said nothing. Instead, she placed the tray on a small folding table in front of the couch and sat down to eat.

When the show ended she clicked off the TV and said, "What do you think about having more than one relationship at a time?"

I waited for her to answer her own question.

"Cat got your tongue, Madison?"

That caught me by surprise. "Sorry."

"Not as sorry as you'll be soon," she said. "How did you find Ethan Landers?"

"He found me."

"Really?" Ms. Skelling sounded surprised. "How . . . resourceful."

"I'm not sure I believe that."

"I was sure the police had him."

"What difference does it make now?"

Again, she seemed to be having a conversation with herself. "What did he tell you?"

A moment of silence passed. Then I said, "Are you asking me?"

"Who else would I be asking?" Ms. Skelling said with a dose of annoyance.

I felt a chill. Did she not realize she had conversations with herself? "He told me you killed his girlfriend and made it look like he did it."

"Megan Woodworth."

"God, wasn't she a piece of work?"

"Thought she walked on water."

"They all do."

"Not anymore."

"So you thought you'd be a hero? You thought you'd come here to rescue your friends? Some friends. I feel sorry for you, Madison. You're so afraid that people only like you for your money. You think you have to be so nice to everyone because it's the only fair way to be when you've been blessed with so much good fortune. What's that fancy phrase for it? *Noblesse oblige?* No wonder you were so fascinated by that little bitch, Courtney. Such a bad girl. You liked that, didn't you?"

"She's different," I said, knowing the best thing I could do was be agreeable and engage her. Maybe, if I could make her feel like I understood her, she would let me and my friends go. "I'd never really known anyone like her."

"We have," Ms. Skelling said. "Dozens of them. Snotty little bitches that think they're the hottest things since sliced bread. Makes us sick."

Us? I thought. *What's she talking about?*

"Don't you think the world would be better off without skanks like that?" she went on. "Who gives them the right to make everyone else feel so miserable?"

"Maybe no one gives it to them?"

"Maybe they just take it because no one stops them."

"Everyone is too scared."

It was hard to understand who she was speaking to.

"Can I ask something?" I said.

Ms. Skelling was silent for a moment, as if considering this request. "What?"

"Usually, the kids who care about that are the ones who, you know, have the problems with it. But you're pretty and sexy. I mean, it's hard to imagine you ever had those kinds of problems."

"What does she know?" Ms. Skelling said. "Should we tell her?"

"What will it matter? We'll be going in a few hours."

"You're right."

"The wonders of cosmetic surgery. Like the old showtune said, 'Tits and ass can change your life.'"

"But that came later. Much later."

"When we were your age we didn't know. We were too scared to even think about it."

"Plain looking, with a nose that was too big and eyes too close together. Flat as a board. A face only a mother could love."

"But not our mother. The double whammy. She hated our looks more than the kids at school."

"Nowhere to run, nowhere to hide."

"They always found us."

"The terror we had to live with."

"The way they stared. The hate in their eyes."

"Even from our own mother, that stupid cruel bitch!"

"It's only fair that they feel what it was like. Only fair that they know."

Their eyes, I thought.

"They should suffer like we did," Ms. Skelling went on. "Feel like trapped animals."

"We did, didn't we?"

She fell silent, gazing off across the room. On the floor I slowly tried to extend my legs again, testing how strong the cords were. Could I break them? And if I did, then what?

Ms. Skelling turned back to me. "Too bad, Madison. You shouldn't be here. These aren't your friends. Couldn't you see that? Do you really think any of them would have come here for you? And now, even if they do, it will be too late."

She finished eating and went back into the kitchen. As soon as she left, I tried to straighten my legs and pulled as hard as I could with my wrists. The rope was too strong. Keeping my eye on the kitchen doorway, I tried again but felt as if I was pulling my shoulders out of their sockets. A new conversation began in the kitchen: "You can't take all this food."

"You expect me to just leave it here?"

"Take the canned goods. Leave the perishables."

"It could be a long trip."

"You'll manage."

"How do you know?"

"You always do."

"What about . . . ?"

"Oh, right." The slippers slapped out of the kitchen again.

"Time for you to leave." Taking hold of the rope from my wrists to my feet, Ms. Skelling dragged me across the floor, through a doorway into the cold, damp air outside, over the cold wet ground to the rough concrete and stink of the pens. The wet quickly soaked through my jeans and hoodie and pressed against my skin. She dragged me past the pen where Ethan lay, his eyes closed, mouth agape, hair matted and dark with blood, a black collar around his neck. She opened a pen and dragged me in. So I was going in a cage like the others. Then was my fate to be like the others as well? She kneeled behind me. My nose filled with the sharp odor of filth. I shivered in the damp cold. From the tugging on the rope I had a feeling she was cutting it. I was so scared. My stomach was in my throat.

"You don't have to do this," I said, trying to sound calm.

"Do what?"

"Put us in these cages. Keep us here. You can go. I promise I'll make the others swear not to tell."

The rope was cut. I felt her tug at some of the strands around my wrists to loosen them. Then the gate clanged shut. I swiveled my head around and watched as she went back into the house.

I sat up and worked my wrists free, then undid the ropes from my ankles. I searched my pockets for my cell phone, but of course, Ms. Skelling had taken it. It was dusk. The sun had gone down, but there was still enough light to see. The cold crept through my clothes and my teeth chattered. The gate to the pen was locked. I turned to the other pens and whispered, "Courtney? Adam?"

No answer.

"Courtney, Adam, it's Madison. Are you in there?"

I heard some scratching sounds. From the doghouse in a pen near mine. Courtney's head came out slowly, her hair a nest of dirt and pieces of brown leaves. Her face looked boney and streaked with grime; her dry lips were cracked, her eyes sunken. Her lips moved and a hoarse whisper came out: "I'm so thirsty."

I looked around. Except for a green hose lying on the ground near the house, there was no source of water. An empty bowl covered with a gross layer of crust lay on the ground in each pen.

Lucy died of dehydration.

"I'm so cold," Courtney whispered. Her teeth were chattering.

I looked around for a way out of these pens but I doubted I'd find one. They looked like they'd been there for a long time.

"Get me out of here, Madison," Courtney whispered.

"I'll try," I whispered back, with no real idea of what to do. "How's Adam?"

Courtney shook her head. "I don't know."

"When did you last see him?"

"I don't know," she whispered. "It's hard to remember."

It was getting darker, and colder. The vapor of our breaths seemed to thicken. The wire fencing went over the tops of the pens. The doors were latched from the outside and wide rectangular metal plates prevented anyone from reaching the latch from inside.

I sat on the hard wet concrete and pulled my knees up against my chest, feeling the vein in my neck beating hard with fear, the dampness soaking in against my butt. Why had I insisted on coming here with Ethan? What had I been thinking? How stupid had I been? By now my mother must have come home. She'd see the broken glass and that my car was gone. She'd call the police first and then Dad in London. Then, while Dad raced in a panic to find a flight home, and the police investigated, she would lock herself alone in her bedroom where no one could see, and silently go hysterical.

How could I be such an idiot?

The cold continued to creep through my clothes, and I shivered uncontrollably.

"Courtney?" I whispered, but she didn't answer. Hoping it might be a little warmer in the doghouse, I crawled inside. The smell made me want to gag and I was glad that in the dark I couldn't see what I was lying on. I just lay there curled in a ball, trembling, unable to sleep, miserable, alone, alternately furious with myself and terrified of what was going to happen next.

Friday 4:46 A.M.

IT WAS EARLY in the morning, maybe an hour before dawn. I'd never been so cold in my life, lying on my side, curled up tight, shivering, my teeth chattering so hard I had to concentrate to keep from biting my tongue. Suddenly there was loud thrashing in the woods nearby, followed by muffled grunts. They sounded human, but I couldn't be sure. Then came more grunts and muttering and the sound of something heavy being dragged through the sticks and leaves.

I got to my hands and knees and peeked out of the doghouse. In the predawn moonlight Ms. Skelling was dragging someone. Her arms went around his chest and she walked backward with his heels scraping the ground. It was too dark to see who it was.

"They're really starting to come out of the woodwork," I heard her say.

"Very funny."

"Seriously, it's time to go."

"I know. There are just a few things left to take care of."

She opened a metal gate, dragged the body into the empty

pen across from mine, and let it fall with a thump. Then the gate clanged shut.

"What happened?" The whisper in the dark caught me by surprise. It was Courtney.

"She caught someone else," I whispered back.

The hour before dawn isn't just the darkest. It is also the coldest and loneliest. I sat up in the doghouse, knees pulled under my chin, teeth chattering, icy tears dripping down my cheeks. The sky was just beginning to grow light when I heard a long, low groan. I looked out. Tyler lay in the pen across from mine. He pushed himself up on one elbow and pressed his hand against his head.

"Tyler?" I whispered.

He looked up sharply, surprise turning into wonder. "Madison? What is this?"

I pressed my finger to my lips, then whispered. "A dog kennel."

Tyler looked over at Ethan, who still lay unconscious. His eyes widened, then narrowed. Somehow I knew that behind his closed lips he was gritting his teeth. "Well, well," he muttered.

"He didn't kill your sister," I said.

Tyler shot me a questioning look. I gave him a brief account of how Ethan had come to my house and told me what had happened and why he'd been on the run.

"You believed him?" Tyler asked dubiously.

"Sometimes you know when someone is telling you the truth. Besides, we know it was Skelling."

Tyler hung his head. I guessed he was realizing that he'd made a mistake. He'd followed Ethan to Soundview, thinking he was the killer. Meanwhile Ethan had followed the real killer here.

Tyler looked up. "What about the others?"

I pointed at a nearby doghouse. "Courtney's in there, dying of thirst. Adam's in even worse shape. I'm so scared, Tyler. I think Skelling's planning to go soon. I don't know if she plans to kill us first or just leave us here to die."

He didn't answer, just looked around as if sizing up the situation.

"How did you find this place?" I asked.

"Maura. So Skelling just leaves you out here until you die of thirst and exposure?"

I wondered if he was thinking about how his sister must have died. The sky slowly continued to brighten. He stared at the latch holding my pen closed. I could tell from his face that he was formulating an idea.

"What is it?" I whispered.

"These pens were built to keep dogs in," he whispered back. "Not people."

"So?"

"Dogs don't know how to help other dogs get free." He crawled into his doghouse. I heard a loud *crack!* and the doghouse shook. Then another *crack!* and another. He was kicking at the wall from inside.

The knob on the door from the house started to turn. "Tyler!" I gasped.

The door flew open and Ms. Skelling stomped out, eyes darting left and right, looking for the source of the sound. In one hand she carried a small black device about the size of a TV remote. In the other was the pipe she'd hit Ethan with. I cowered in my doghouse as she walked between the two rows of pens, her head swinging back and forth. She stared in at me, then turned and poked the pipe at Tyler's doghouse. "Come out!"

Tyler stuck his head out of the doghouse, pretending to blink and yawn as if he'd been asleep.

"Did you make that noise?" Ms. Skelling asked.

He shook his head and pointed at me.

"No!" I gasped. Ms. Skelling pressed a button on the device in her hand. The jolt felt as if someone had kicked me in the neck, knocking me back and making me cry out. Through eyes quickly filling with tears, I stared up at her blurred image.

"Whatever you were doing, don't do it again," Ms. Skelling threatened. "Next time will be five times worse."

Tears spilled out of my eyes. I felt totally betrayed. Why had Tyler pointed at me? He had to know what Ms. Skelling would do. Meanwhile, the madwoman moved to the pen where Ethan lay on the ground. She stuck the pipe through the fence and poked him. Ethan moaned slightly but hardly moved. Next she stepped to Courtney's pen and banged the pipe against the doghouse. Courtney peered out, shivering and trembling. "I need water," she rasped.

"Of course you do," Ms. Skelling replied with fake sympathy. "I'll get you something to drink very soon."

She turned to the pen where Adam lay and poked at him. "Wake up."

I heard the dull thud of the pipe against flesh but no response of any kind. Not even a groan.

"Wake up!" Ms. Skelling prodded him harder.

Through my tears I saw her reach for the control and heard the spitting sound of the electric collar. But Adam didn't flinch.

"Well, well," Ms. Skelling muttered, opening the pen. "Just in time."

I started sobbing harder. *Not Adam! Oh, please! Not Adam!*

The next thing I knew, Ms. Skelling was dragging Adam's body past my pen. I tried not to look. I heard the door to the house open, and she dragged his body inside. I was still sobbing, for Adam, and out of shock and fear and confusion by what Tyler had done.

I heard the sound of wood creaking and looked out. Tyler was squatting outside his doghouse, trying to work a slat from the bottom. He must have been trying to loosen it by kicking from the inside. He noticed me.

"Sorry about that," he whispered, wedging his fingers behind the loose slat. "I had to divert her attention before she noticed."

It still seemed like a terrible thing to do, but at least I understood. Tyler pulled harder at the slat and it made a creaking sound.

"She'll hear you," I whispered, using my sleeve to dab away the tears.

"So? Better this than just wait here to die. There's no way she's just going to leave us behind."

"How do you know?"

"Because they're called serial killers, not serial leave-victims-behind-to-help-testify-against-them. Keep an eye on the door."

Even though my neck still throbbed from the shock, and I was still angry at him, I knew he was right. Tyler managed to work the slat away from the doghouse. It was just narrow enough to fit through the fence around his pen, and long enough to reach to the front of my pen. I couldn't see what he was doing, but I could hear squeaks and clinks as he tried to undo the latch.

The doorknob started to turn.

"She's coming!" I whispered.

Tyler had just enough time to pull the slat back through the fence and press it against the doghouse. Before he could crawl back inside, Ms. Skelling was there, eyes narrowed suspiciously. "You're up to something." She reached for her belt.

"Ahhhh!" Tyler twisted into an uncontrollable spasm that left him sprawled on the floor of the pen. I could tell from the sound of the shock that it had been much stronger than the one she had given me.

"That should do it."

"Indeed it should."

"We'll have no more trouble from that one." She went back into the house. Tyler lay on the ground, his chest heaving.

"Are you okay?" I whispered.

"Holy crap . . ." He groaned hoarsely and tried to sit up. The side of his face was covered with filth from the pen. Suddenly he went pale, leaned to the side, and threw up. "Fricken sadist." He wiped his mouth with his sleeve, his hand on his neck where she'd shocked him. But a moment later he picked up the slat again and stuck it through the fencing toward the latch on my pen.

I kept my eyes on the door, but now and then glanced at Tyler. His skin was ashen. Despite risking an even more devastating shock next time, he was totally focused on what he was doing.

Clink! The sound that came from the latch on my pen was

loud and metallic. Even as Tyler pulled the slat back through the fencing, the door to the house was swinging open. Tyler barely had time to press the slat against the bottom of the doghouse before Ms. Skelling was there, her hand already reaching for her belt.

Zap! Tyler let out a shriek and convulsed on the ground. Meanwhile, Ms. Skelling studied his pen intently, as if searching for a clue as to what he'd been doing. Finding nothing, she finally turned and went back inside.

Tyler lay on the floor of the pen, his chest rising and falling in rapid, short breaths. A burnt scent reached my nose and I recoiled at the realization that it was the smell of scorched flesh. She'd shocked him so hard the skin had burned.

I also realized how Ms. Skelling had come out so quickly. She'd been waiting and listening on the other side of the kitchen door. That chatter about having no more trouble from that one had been a ploy, a setup to try and catch Tyler red-handed.

I waited, not sure what to do. Because of the loud clinking sound, and the way Tyler had started to pull back the slat even before Skelling raced out of the house, I had a feeling the latch on the door of my pen was open. But now what? Did I dare try it and risk making a sound that might bring Ms. Skelling out again? What else could I do? Just sit there and wait for her to kill us all? Still I waited, praying Tyler would come to.

It seemed like Tyler lay on the cold, wet ground for a long time, but maybe it only felt long because of how frightened I was. I kept looking back at the door to the house. Was Ms. Skelling on the other side, still listening? Even if she wasn't, how long would it be before she came back? In his pen, Tyler's hands slowly closed into fists. He struggled to push himself up on his elbows, then seemed to lose strength, and collapsed again.

Please get up, Tyler, I prayed. *Please!*

As if he heard me, he once again struggled to his elbows. The effort seemed to exhaust him, and he stayed like that for a while. Then he slowly sat up and looked at me. His eyes were glassy and dull. His dirty cheeks were streaked with tears, and blood dripped from the corner of his mouth.

"You're bleeding," I whispered.

His forehead bunched. He pressed the back of his hand against his mouth and it came away red. "Bit my tongue pretty bad." His words were garbled, as if he'd just come from having a tooth filled at the dentist.

"Now what?" I whispered.

Tyler blinked rapidly as if he needed a moment to remember where he was. His eyes focused. "Go get help."

Just get up, push open the gate, and run? It was questionable whether I'd be able to get away without Ms. Skelling seeing me. And even if I did, by the time I got to my car, found someplace where I could call for help, and waited for help to come, she was sure to have noticed I was gone. And then she would kill Courtney, Tyler, and Ethan—if he wasn't already dead—and quickly take off.

Tyler stared at me and again urged, "Go!"

Trembling with fear, I shook my head. I didn't want to go. I didn't want to die, but I wasn't sure I could live with myself if I ran away.

"What are you doing?" Tyler whispered. He must have been

incredibly frustrated that I wasn't going for help after he'd suffered so much pain to win my freedom.

"I don't know," I whispered back, my eyes filling with tears of fright. "I don't want to go. She'll catch me. And even if I get away, she'll kill you and Courtney and Ethan."

"What good is staying going to do?" Tyler asked.

"I don't know." I was racked with confusion and fear.

"You can't fight her," Tyler said. "The second she sees you, she'll zap you." But even as the words came out of his mouth, his eyes changed as if he'd just thought of something. "Why didn't I think of this sooner?" he muttered and pointed at my doghouse. "Tear off a piece of shingle. A thick piece, about an inch square. Slide it between your neck and the prongs. Then cover it with your hair."

I did as I was told. The shingles were old and crumbly. It was easy to tear off a corner. "Now what?" I whispered.

There wasn't time for Tyler to answer. The door opened and Ms. Skelling came out again. She saw us facing each other in our pens and must have instantly suspected we were hatching a plan. She reached for her belt and Tyler cried out and was sent sprawling. Then she turned to me.

The pressure of the jolt was like someone slapping me on the neck with a ruler but nothing more. Still, I let out a yelp and sprawled on the ground as if the shock had hit me full force. The piece of shingle felt hot against my neck. Out of the corner of my eye, I watched Ms. Skelling continue down the pens and open Ethan's.

I looked across at Tyler. His face lay against the dirt, eyes closed, blood dribbling out of his mouth. I had to do something, but what? I looked back at the house. The shovel and hayfork were leaning against the wall.

I heard a grunt. Ms. Skelling was backing out of Ethan's pen with her arms under his shoulders, dragging him. My heart was racing, my forehead felt tight and hot, and my breaths were so shallow and fast that I felt light-headed. I don't think I ever felt so scared. But what was the point of waiting? I opened my pen gate as quietly as possible, then rushed toward the house.

The wooden handle of the hayfork felt heavy and cold in my trembling hands. I turned and went back into the kennel. Still dragging Ethan, Ms. Skelling had her back to me. I stopped and waited, holding the hayfork out in front of me. As Ms. Skelling dragged Ethan past my pen, she saw the open gate and stopped. She twisted her head around.

She stared at me with the slightest scowl, as if wondering how I'd managed to escape. My heart was banging out of control, and I was trembling. I'm sure she saw that. Her scowl slowly became an evil, knowing smile. She let Ethan drop to the ground, and reached for her belt.

I felt a light jolt at my neck and the shingle grew hot. Ms. Skelling frowned deeply and pressed the button again. Another jolt and the shingle grew so hot it practically burned my skin, but I knew I couldn't take it away. Ms. Skelling sneered and reached for the pipe.

I was no longer trembling. Now I was shaking, almost uncontrollably. I felt the urge to cry for help. That's what I'd been able to do all my life, and someone—my mother, my father, a friend—had always come. But what good would crying for help do now?

I wanted to drop the hayfork and run, but I knew I wouldn't get far. And that left only one choice. I had one chance, and that was to stand and fight. It wasn't much of a chance. I'd managed, my whole life, to avoid fighting. But now this hayfork was all I had. It was all that stood between me and certain death.

Ms. Skelling came toward me. She was bigger and stronger, and she had no reluctance about using that pipe. There wasn't a doubt in my mind that she was looking forward to using it in the most horrible ways imaginable. I gripped the handle of the hayfork. *One more step*, I thought, *and you have to do it.*

For Courtney, and Lucy, and Adam.

And all the others.

And for yourself.

She took that step. We locked eyes. Hers were wide but strangely blank, almost as if someone were operating her body by remote control.

I squeezed the handle of the hayfork and—

Just at that moment, Ms. Skelling fell.

I heard the thud and the grunt. Ms. Skelling was on her hands and knees just a few feet away. On the ground just behind her was the slat from Tyler's doghouse.

He'd used it to trip her. Still sprawled on the ground, he looked up at me, his face contorted with pain and covered with dirt and blood.

Ms. Skelling also looked up at me. The pipe had flown from her hand and lay on the ground between us.

"Madison, do it!" Tyler rasped.

Shaking, more terrified than I'd ever been in my entire life, I took a step forward, gesturing threateningly with the hayfork. The sharp prongs were less than a foot from Ms. Skelling's face. But it felt like an empty, feeble gesture. It was one thing to defend myself if she were attacking, but now her weapon was gone and she was on her hands and knees. . . .

"For God's sake!" Tyler pleaded.

Ms. Skelling looked up at me, her eyes no longer blank. Now they were filled with reason and sincerity. "Don't listen to him, Madison. You don't have to do it. I'll let you and your friends go. Just give me a few hours to get away. You can give Courtney water. Just promise me you'll give me a few hours. You're a good girl, Madison. I know you'd never break a promise."

She was lying, and we both knew it. She wasn't about to let me go.

"I swear to you," Ms. Skelling said. "You have my word. Let me go and nothing bad will happen to any of you."

I glanced at Tyler. He lay on the floor of the pen, his eyes filled with terror and his mouth open, either too exhausted or in too much pain to speak. I looked back at Ms. Skelling and said, "You're not going anywhere. I want you to give yourself up. We're going to find a phone and call the police."

Ms. Skelling hesitated, then said, "All right."

"I want you to get up . . . very slowly."

Ms. Skelling stared up at me. Hands still on the ground, she started to rise, pulling her feet under her. Suddenly her hand darted toward the pipe.

I jabbed the hayfork forward, stopping just inches from her face.

"I won't!" she gasped, jerking her hand back. "I'm sorry. Really! I can't always control it. If I could, I wouldn't be this way in the first place."

Still trembling—from the cold, the fear, the terrible thought of what I might have to do—I held the hayfork level with her eyes. Crouched on the ground, Ms. Skelling stared up at me, a puzzled, almost curious expression on her face, as if she didn't understand why I didn't just do it.

She slowly started to rise. "You don't want to do it, do you? You don't want to hurt me. You've never wanted to hurt anyone. That's why everyone likes you so much, Madison. It's why I like you, too. It's why you were never one of the ones we singled out. It's why I won't hurt you now. I swear you can trust me, Madison. I know what we've done is terrible and evil. I know we're sick. Horribly sick."

She was standing now. I held the hayfork, aimed at her stomach. Ms. Skelling's right hand began to slowly move toward the tines of the hayfork and gently but firmly pushed them aside. "You see?" she said calmly. "We're not going to hurt you. And we're not going to hurt your friends." She placed her hand on the handle of the hayfork. "You can let go, Madison. It's all right."

I felt her take hold of the hayfork handle, could feel her start to ease it away from me. I didn't want to kill her. I wanted her to give herself up.

Don't let her . . . , a voice in my head said. I saw Lucy, Adam, and Courtney. My mother and father. They all knew. It was their voices I heard. My hands tightened on the handle.

Ms. Skelling felt the resistance. Her eyes narrowed and

suddenly she pulled hard, trying to yank the hayfork out of my grip. But I didn't let go.

It was a tug-of war-now, with Ms. Skelling holding the hayfork handle near the tine end, and me on the other end. Ms. Skelling yanked. "Let go!"

But I held on. For dear life.

"I said, let go!" Ms. Skelling yanked again.

"You have to give yourself up," I said, still holding tight.

"Yeah, right," she scoffed.

"I mean it!"

"You couldn't hurt a fly, you wimp!" Ms. Skelling snarled and pulled hard on the hayfork.

This time I didn't resist. I jabbed the hayfork as hard as I could.

Ms. Skelling stumbled backward and slammed into one of the pens.

The hayfork kept going. . . .

Ms. Skelling's eyes widened and her mouth fell open. She stared down at the hayfork buried deep in her middle, at the red stains growing around the tines. Then she looked up at me. "You . . . little . . . bitch."

"Damn right," I said.

chapter 22

I CALLED 911, then brought water out for Courtney. Ethan was still unconscious on the kennel floor, but his heart was beating. When the police arrived, I was sitting with Tyler's head in my lap, just holding him.

The police would eventually establish that Joyce Carol Alberti—age 47, aka Mary Louise Smith, Rhonda Petersen, Carol Skelling, and IaMnEmEsIs—was responsible for at least seven deaths in five states. All the victims were considered popular kids and all lived in "nice, safe, well-to-do" suburbs like Soundview, the last places on earth where anyone imagined something like that happening.

But it indeed happened, and more sadness would follow. Lucy's funeral was held three days later. Adam's, two days after that. School closed and everyone went and cried for days afterward. Even today it's still indescribably sad. Life in Soundview will never be the same.

The blow to Ethan's skull caused some slight brain damage. His parents took him back to Shawnee Mission, and he's getting all kinds of treatments and therapy. We send each other a Face-book message now and then, and he tells me he's getting better.

Courtney recovered completely. Her mother came back from India. They fight a lot about her curfew.

Maura hasn't come back to school, and I've heard she's moving away. I sent her a message saying that it wasn't her fault and nobody blames her. But she didn't write back.

At low tide, the seagulls picked up clams and dropped them on the seawall behind my house. It was a cold, clear December afternoon, and I sat on a bench in our backyard, watching the gulls and enjoying the warmth of the sun on my face.

Suddenly I felt the presence of someone behind me.

Tensing, I swiveled around.

It was Tyler. The momentary fright drained out of me, and I smiled.

"Your mom said I'd find you back here," he said.

I patted the bench beside me and he sat down, leaning forward and resting his elbows on his knees. For a few moments we watched a gull peck at a clam in a broken shell.

"I always think seagulls have to be pretty smart to break open clams by dropping them," I finally said.

"Not as smart as the ones in Kansas City," said Tyler.

"Why's that?"

"In KC they just hang around in the parking lot at McDonald's."

I glanced out of the corner of my eye at him. "Are there really seagulls in Kansas City?"

"I can let you know, if you'd like."

I felt my heart sink. He'd come to say good-bye. He was going home. "What about finishing high school?"

"I graduated two years ago, Madison."

Yes, I thought sadly. *I should have guessed.* "I always thought you seemed more mature than other guys. Didn't your parents wonder where you were?"

"I told them I was living in the city, staying with friends and working as a bartender. That's the funny thing about cell phones. People never really know where you are."

A gull dropped another clam. We watched the small white dot drop against the blue sky background and shatter on the wall. "Bull's-eye," Tyler said.

"I have another question," I said. "If Ms. Skelling taught at your school, didn't you know her?"

He shook his head. "She must have started there the year after I graduated. I guess you've probably figured out by now that I'm not the kind of guy who'd go back to visit."

I nodded.

"I've got a question for you," he said. "You ever figure out who PBleeker was?"

I nodded again. "I've promised not to tell."

It *was* Dave. He'd told me at Adam's funeral and apologized. I'd recalled that day in the library when I'd asked him if he was PBleeker, and how convincing his denial had been. Maybe I just wasn't that good at reading people.

"Did I hear you've applied to Tufts early decision?" Tyler asked.

"Yes."

"Your parents okay with that? I mean, after everything that's happened?"

"They wanted me to stay closer, but I have to get away . . . from the memories."

A gull rose in the air and dropped another clam.

"Don't they ever miss?" Tyler asked.

"Sometimes. When it's windy . . . What do you think you'll do back in Kansas City?"

"Spend some time with my parents. I heard that the police searched Skelling's house and found some information about what she did with Megan. I don't think my parents ever gave up hope that she was still alive, so I have to go back and be with them now."

The air was still and the water glassy. The Sound was like a giant pond. I gazed out across it. A tugboat was pulling a barge, leaving an ever-widening wake. I wanted to tell Tyler that I wished he wouldn't go, but I couldn't. He had to go back and comfort his parents.

"Madison?"

"Yes?"

"I'll probably have to stay out in KC for a few months, but it won't be forever. Frank says that any time I want to come back to the garage in the spring, there'll be a job for me. So I was just wondering . . . if that was something you thought you might approve of?"

I felt a smile on my lips and slid my hand into his. "Yes, Tyler, I think I would."